Introduction

One of the standard interview questions for candidates seeking a job in the BBC arts department, a producer once told me, invites suggestions for contributors to a documentary about the history of the British Museum. Apart from famous curators and archae-ologists, the potential voice most commonly offered is, apparently, that of David Lodge. This anecdotal evidence shows the extent to which the title of his third novel obeys, in the minds of students of English, the verb shared with his surname.

If, however, in 1965, the author had been able, like some Catholic saint or mystic, to see his future, he would surely have been astonished at the idea that *The British Museum is Falling Down* might one day lodge in a list of classic titles. In an afterword to a new edition of the novel in 1981, the writer outlined the various catastrophes attending its first appearance.

His original title had been *The British Museum Had Lost Its Charm*, taken from a 1937 song by George and Ira Gershwin, 'A Foggy Day (in London Town)'. This lyric, a hit for both Fred Astaire and Ella Fitzgerald, was, Lodge says, one of his inspir-ations for the fact that his story plays out within a single day. But the Gershwin estate refused him permission to use the line and the novelist regarded as a poor substitution the title which we are now celebrating in 2010.

Even when this replacement name was safely stamped on the jacket of the MacGibbon & Kee first edition, the novel seemed to remain the opposite of charmed. Although it is not uncommon for reviews of a new book to appear intermittently and distantly from the publication date, Lodge's novel, in the weeks after its release in October 1965, went completely unnoticed. This, it turned out, was the fault not of literary editors but of either publisher or Post Office: for reasons never discovered, review copies had never reached the intended literary offices and so it was given a second, emergency release weeks after the first.

A book which found it so hard to be born has, though, enjoyed a happy and vibrant life. Four and a half decades on, Lodge's *British Museum* has certainly maintained its charm.

It is now, in two senses, a period piece. By the time of the book's publication, five years after Penguin won in court the right to publish D. H. Lawrence's *Lady Chatterley's Lover*, most aspects of sexual practice had been covered by fiction. Lodge, though, introduced to fiction what was, in moral terms, an entirely novel sexual position: the requirement for Catholic couples, banned from using pharmaceutical or barrier methods of birth control, to monitor the wife's menstrual cycle in order to find times in which conception was least likely to occur. The idea of making love only during the sanctified nights of the so-called 'Safe Period', or 'natural family planning' – phrases which turned out to be as misleading as 'friendly fire' and 'efficiency savings' – would have seemed bizarre to non-Catholic readers at the time. Now it will read as a variety of erotic science fiction even to members of Pope Benedict XVI's flock, as most Catholics – outside, perhaps, of the more pious parts of Ireland – long ago concluded that the authority of priests did not reach the bedroom.

This lapsing of the narrative's central premise might have doomed the book's chances of durability. Lodge, though, took precautions against his book becoming redundant by practising natural mirth control. Although this is now a historical novel – in terms of not only Catholics and sex but also the necessity, improbable to younger readers, of putting coins into a box like Dr Who's to make a phone call – Lodge, as good contemporary novelists do, has provided enough physical detail for the work now to serve as social history.

The British Museum is
Falling Down

DAVID LODGE

PENGUIN BOOKS

PENGUIN BOOKS

Published by the Penguin Group
Penguin Books Ltd, 80 Strand, London WC2R ORL, England
Penguin Group (USA), Inc., 375 Hudson Street, New York, New York 10014, USA
Penguin Group (Canada), 90 Eglinton Avenue East, Suite 700, Toronto, Ontario, Canada M4P 2Y3
(a division of Pearson Penguin Canada Inc.)
Penguin Ireland, 25 St Stephen's Green, Dublin 2, Ireland (a division of Penguin Books Ltd)
Penguin Group (Australia), 250 Camberwell Road, Camberwell, Victoria 3124, Australia
(a division of Pearson Australia Group Pty Ltd)
Penguin Books India Pvt Ltd, 11 Community Centre, Panchsheel Park, New Delhi – 110 017, India
Penguin Group (NZ), 67 Apollo Drive, Rosedale, North Shore 0632, New Zealand
(a division of Pearson New Zealand Ltd)
Penguin Books (South Africa) (Pty) Ltd, 24 Sturdee Avenue, Rosebank,
Johannesburg 2196, South Africa

Penguin Books Ltd, Registered Offices: 80 Strand, London WC2R ORL, England

www.penguin.com

First published by MacGibbon & Kee 1965
Published in Penguin Books 1983
Reissued with a new introduction in Penguin Books 2010

1

Copyright © David Lodge, 1965
Introduction copyright © Mark Lawson, 2010

The moral right of the author and of the introducer has been asserted

All rights reserved
Without limiting the rights under copyright
reserved above, no part of this publication may be
reproduced, stored in or introduced into a retrieval system,
or transmitted, in any form or by any means (electronic, mechanical,
photocopying, recording or otherwise), without the prior
written permission of both the copyright owner and
the above publisher of this book

Set in 11/13 Dante MT
Typeset by Ellipsis Books Limited, Glasgow
Printed in Great Britain by Clays Ltd, St Ives plc

A CIP catalogue record for this book is available from the British Library

ISBN: 978-0-141-04669-3

www.greenpenguin.co.uk

Mixed Sources
Product group from well-managed
forests and other controlled sources
www.fsc.org Cert no. SA-COC-1592
© 1996 Forest Stewardship Council

Penguin Books is committed to a sustainable future
for our business, our readers and our planet.
The book in your hands is made from paper
certified by the Forest Stewardship Council.

The British Museum is Falling Down is fascinating as a counter-point to the standard version of the 1960s as an era in which the Pill made sex free of fret or consequence; Lodge's Adam and Barbara Appleby have the terrible poignancy of people diagnosed as diabetics just as the government starts handing out free chocolate rations. Infidelity had become such a standard fictional plot-twist that, by the 1970s, 'Hampstead adultery novel' was used as a term of critical abuse, but Adam's temptation in the ninth chapter of this book is surely the only illicit sex scene in literature to involve a thermometer and the suggestion of a three-week delay before coitus.

The comedy of sex, though, is only part of the pleasure. The novel's pivotal phrase occurs when Adam complains, 'Literature is mostly about having sex and not much about having children. Life is the other way round.'

With pleasing structural subtlety, the text ensures that the protagonist, who is denied any sex during its 173 pages, achieves multiple entries into literature. As the 1981 afterword advises, 'There are ten passages of parody or pastiche in the novel.' The writer was discouraged by the editor of the English first edition from flagging the presence of these parodies on the dust jacket and most reviewers apparently failed to spot them. This seems a failure of criticism because, though I have admittedly always read the book alerted to their presence, Lodge generally winks at the reader during the passages when he is writing in disguise. During the Lawrentian parody, Adam helpfully thinks about D. H. Lawrence, while the opening paragraph of the sequence of departmental intrigue which apes the novels of C. P. Snow nudges us with a double-edged weather report: 'It looked like snow.'

There are also, for readers with a thorough knowledge of any of the models, deeper, quieter details. The pages of Graham Greene pastiche begin with Adam passing a 'green baize door', a phrase which not only plants the surname of the novelist who is under-writing this stretch but, more specifically, is Greene's own description of the portal between the school and family premises at Berkhamsted School, where his father was headmaster. Consistently crossing this barrier into 'another country' (another phrase Lodge drops in) was, Greene claimed, the experience which made him a writer and a spy.

The question arises for the writer of this introduction – much as it did for Lodge's first publisher – of how much of a map should be given to the book's sub-terrain of imitation. The author, in that 1981 afterword, listed the models in alphabetical order. What I suggest is that anyone who doesn't want to know – or wishes to compare checklists later – should, as they say during the football results at the end of the news, look away now. The impersonations occur in this order: Virginia Woolf (Chapter Two), Franz Kafka, D. H. Lawrence, Joseph Conrad (Chapter Three), C. P. Snow (Chapter Four), Fr. Rolfe / Baron Corvo's Hadrian VII and Henry James (Chapter Five), Graham Greene (Chapter Six), Ernest Hemingway (Chapter Seven), James Joyce (Epilogue). There's also a bit of Evelyn Waugh in the second chapter, a lot of Kingsley Amis in the eighth and various other more passing glances to literary traditions.

In a later Lodge novel, *How Far Can You Go?* (1980), Catholic students studying English at London University in the 1950s take pride from the power of the papist novel, then represented by Graham Greene, Evelyn Waugh, Muriel Spark and Anthony Burgess. One undergraduate says of Greene and Waugh: 'It said in *The Observer* that they're the two best English novelists going, so that's one in the eye for the Prods.' By the time I was a (Roman Catholic) school and college English student in the 1970s and early 80s, David Lodge had himself joined the aforementioned holy quartet as a source of literary pride and affirmation for Catholics.

And, appropriately for a book so concerned with conception, this novel can now be seen to contain the seeds of several later key Lodge works. The tragi-comedy of the snakes-and-ladders game of Roman Catholic moral teaching was expanded in *How Far Can You Go?* A fascination with transatlantic misunderstandings – an American caller to the British Museum is thrown by the operator's use of the phrase 'You're through', words introductory in Britain, valedictory in the US – bloomed magnificently in the campus swap story *Changing Places* (1975). And the Henry James parody which closes Chapter Five of *The British Museum is Falling Down* can be seen as a warm-up exercise for the much later fictionalized biography of James, *Author, Author* (2004).

More broadly, Adam Appleby's determination that his future lies in a university also applies to Lodge's fiction: five of his next six novels would feature college teachers as central characters, giving Lodge his primary critical identification as a writer of the 'campus novel', the genre affectionately sent up in Chapter Eight of this book, which, as Lodge acknowledges in his 1981 afterword, had been established in Britain by his friend Malcolm Bradbury with the college novel *Eating People Is Wrong* (1959).

Bradbury, though later to become most celebrated as the chief of a pioneering creative writing course at the University of East Anglia, was a teaching colleague of Lodge's at Birmingham in the early 1960s. Lodge has credited friendship – and collaboration on a stage revue – with Bradbury for releasing a comic and playful side in his writing. This novel's immediate successor, *Out of the Shelter*, would return to the social realism of the earlier books, but all his other subsequent fiction was closer to the comic and postmodern style of *The British Museum is Falling Down*.

Most of those novels – giving the author his first experience of prize nominations and televisations – would gain more readers and attention than the novel which follows these words, but David Lodge has admitted to a 'special fondness' for it and the feeling is shared by this reader.

The expression 'catholic with a small c' entered the English language to differentiate between the religious delineation and the word's other meaning of universality. But, in *The British Museum is Falling Down*, a novel packed with shadowings of language, David Lodge did the linguistic double: Catholic and catholic, this winning comedy of 'Vatican Roulette' gives parochial concerns a universal appeal.

Mark Lawson

To Derek Todd
(in affectionate memory of B M days)
and to Malcolm Bradbury
(whose fault it mostly is that I have tried
to write a comic novel)

Life imitates art.

Oscar Wilde

I would be a Papist if I could. I have fear enough, but an obstinate rationality prevents me.

Dr Johnson

I

There were moments of happiness in the British Museum
reading-room, but the body called him back.

Graham Greene

It was Adam Appleby's misfortune that at the moment of
awakening from sleep his consciousness was immediately
flooded with everything he least wanted to think about. Other
men, he gathered, met each new dawn with a refreshed mind
and heart, full of optimism and resolution; or else they moved
sluggishly through the first hour of the day in a state of blessed
numbedness, incapable of any thought at all, pleasant or unpleasant. But, crouched like harpies round his bed, unpleasant
thoughts waited to pounce the moment Adam's eyelids flickered
apart. At that moment he was forced, like a drowning man, to
review his entire life instantaneously, divided between regrets
for the past and fears for the future.

Thus it was that as he opened his eyes one November morning, and focused them blearily on the sick rose, three down
and six across, on the wallpaper opposite his bed, Adam was
simultaneously reminded that he was twenty-five years of age,
and would soon be twenty-six, that he was a postgraduate
student preparing a thesis which he was unlikely to complete
in this the third and final year of his scholarship, that the latter
was hugely overdrawn, that he was married with three very
young children, that one of them had manifested an alarming
rash the previous evening, that his name was ridiculous, that his

leg hurt, that his decrepit scooter had failed to start the previous morning and would no doubt fail to start this morning, that he had just missed a first-class degree because of a bad Middle English paper, that his leg hurt, that at his primary school he had proved so proficient in the game of who-can-pee-highest-up-the-wall of the boys' outside lavatory that he had wetted the biretta of the parish priest who happened to be visiting the playground on the other side of the wall at the time, that he had forgotten to reserve any books at the British Museum for this morning's reading, that his leg hurt, that his wife's period was three days overdue, and that his leg hurt.

But wait a minute . . . One of these mental events was unfamiliar. He could not recall any sensation of pain in his leg on retiring the previous night. And it was not, he reflected bitterly, as if he had enjoyed any strenuous physical activity *after* retiring. When Barbara's period was overdue, neither of them felt much inclination for sex. The thought of another pregnancy had a dampening effect on desire, even though they knew the issue must be already settled, one way or another, in Barbara's womb. At the thought of that womb plumping with another life, a spasm of cold terror coursed through Adam's bowels. In a year's time he should, with luck, have completed his Ph.D. and obtained some kind of job. It was essential that they should avoid conceiving another child at least until then. And if possible for ever.

How different it must be, he thought, the life of an ordinary, non-Catholic parent, free to decide – actually to *decide*, in calm confidence – whether to have or not to have a child. How different from his own married state, which Adam symbolized as a small, over-populated, low-lying island ringed by a crumbling dyke which he and his wife struggled hopelessly to repair as they kept anxious watch on the surging sea of fertility that surrounded them. It was not that, having produced the three children, he and Barbara would now, given the opportunity, actually will them back into non-existence, but this acceptance of new life was not infinitely elastic. Its extension had limits, and Adam thought they had now been reached, at least for the foreseeable future.

His mind turned, as it not infrequently did, to the circumstances which had brought them to this pass. Their marriage more than four years ago had been a hurried affair, precipitated by the announcement that Adam, who was doing his National Service after graduation, was to be posted to Singapore. Shortly afterwards he had proved to be suffering from an ear condition which had restricted him to home postings. This had been a source of joy to them at the time, but in gloomy moments Adam wondered retrospectively whether it had been altogether fortunate. In spite of, or perhaps because of being widely separated – he in Yorkshire and Barbara with her parents in Birmingham – and coming together only on weekend leaves, they had managed to produce two children during his army service.

They had embarked on marriage with vague notions about the Safe Period and a hopeful trust in Providence that Adam now found difficult to credit. Clare had been born nine months after the wedding. Barbara had then consulted a Catholic doctor who gave her a simple mathematical formula for calculating the Safe Period – so simple that Dominic was born one year after Clare. Shortly afterwards Adam was released from the Army, and returned to London to do research. Someone gave Barbara a booklet explaining how she could determine the time of her ovulation by recording her temperature each morning, and they followed this procedure until Barbara became pregnant again.

After Edward's birth they had simply abstained from intercourse for six months of mounting neurosis. Having managed, with some difficulty, to enter the married state as virgins after three years' courtship, they found it hard that they should have to revert to this condition while sharing the same bed. A few months ago they had applied for help to a Catholic Marriage counselling organization, whose doctors had poured a kindly

3

scorn on their amateurish attempts to operate the basal temperature method. They had been given sheets of graph paper and little pieces of cardboard with transparent windows of cellophane to place over the graphs, and recommended, for maximum security, to keep to the post-ovulatory period.

For three anxious months they had survived. Unfortunately, Barbara's ovulation seemed to occur late in her monthly cycle, and their sexual relations were forced into a curious pattern: three weeks of patient graph-plotting, followed by a few nights of frantic lovemaking, which rapidly petered out in exhaustion and renewed suspense. This behaviour was known as Rhythm and was in accordance with the Natural Law.

From the next room came a muffled thump and a sharp cry, which modulated into a low whining that Adam attributed hesitantly to his youngest child, Edward. He glanced sideways at his wife. She lay on her stomach, sucking a thermometer. A small peak in the bedclothes further down indicated the presence of a second thermometer. Unable to decide on the relative accuracy of the oral and rectal methods of taking her temperature, Barbara had decided to employ both. Which would be all right as long as she could be relied upon not to confuse the two readings. Which Adam doubted.

Catching his eye, Barbara muttered something rendered unrecognizable as a human utterance by the presence of the thermometer, but which Adam interpreted as, 'Make a cup of tea.' An interesting example of the function of predictability in casual speech, he mentally observed, as he pulled back the bedclothes. The lino greeted his feet with an icy chill, and he pranced awkwardly round the room on tiptoe, looking for his slippers. It was difficult, he found, to limp and walk on tiptoe at the same time. He discovered his slippers at last in his shirt-drawer, a minute plastic doll made in Hong Kong nestling in the toe of each. He hurriedly donned his dressing-gown. There was a distinct nip in the air: winter was contending with autumn. It made him think of electricity bills. So, when he looked out of the window, did Battersea Power Station, looming vaguely through the morning fog.

After filling and switching on the electric kettle in the kitchen, Adam made his way to the bathroom. But his eldest child had forestalled him.

'I'm passing a motion,' Clare announced.

'Who else is voting?' he cracked uneasily. In theory, Adam fully supported his wife's determination to teach the children an adult vocabulary for their physical functions. But it still disconcerted him – perhaps because it was not a vocabulary he had ever used himself, even as an adult. And it seemed to him positively dangerous to encourage the articulacy of a child so precociously fascinated by physiology as Clare. When Barbara had been in labour with Edward, and a kindly neighbour had hinted archly, 'I think you're going to have a baby brother or sister,' Clare had replied: 'I think so too – the contractions are coming every two minutes.' Such feats were the source of a certain pride in Adam, but he couldn't help thinking that Clare was missing something of the magic and mystery of childhood.

'What's voting?' asked his daughter.

'Will you be long?' he countered.

'I don't know. You just can't tell with these things.'

'Well, don't be long, please. Daddy wants to use the lavatory.'

'Why don't you use Dominic's pot?'

'Daddies don't use pots.'

'Why don't they?'

At a loss for an answer, Adam retreated to the kitchen. Where he had gone wrong, of course, was in categorically denying that Daddies used pots. Daddies often used pots. Eighty per cent of the rural dwellings in Ireland had no sanitation of any kind, for example. The correct gambit would have been: '*I* don't use pots.' Or, better still: '*You* don't use pots any more, do you, Clare?'

The kettle began to boil. Adam suddenly wondered whether he had over-estimated the function of predictability in casual speech. Supposing Barbara had not said, 'Make a cup of tea', but 'Edward has fallen out of his cot', or 'My rectal thermometer is stuck'? He hastened back to the bedroom, pausing only to peep into the children's room to assure himself of Edward's safety. He was quite all right – placidly eating strips of wallpaper which Dominic was tearing off the wall. Adam made Edward spit them out and, holding the moist pulp in his outstretched hand, proceeded to the bedroom.

'You *did* want me to make a cup of tea?' he inquired, putting his head round the door.

Barbara took the thermometer from her mouth and squinted at it. 'Yes,' she said, and replaced the thermometer.

Adam returned to the kitchen, disposed of the pulp and made the tea. While waiting for it to draw he mentally composed a short article, *'Catholicism, Roman*, for a Martian encyclopaedia compiled after life on earth had been destroyed by atomic warfare.

Roman Catholicism was, according to archaeological evidence, distributed fairly widely over the planet Earth in the twentieth century. As far as the Western Hemisphere is concerned, it appears to have been characterized by a complex system of sexual taboos and rituals. Intercourse between married partners was restricted to certain limited periods determined by the calendar and the body-temperature of the female. Martian archaeologists have learned to identify the domiciles of Roman Catholics by the presence of large numbers of complicated graphs, calendars, small booklets full of figures, and quantities of broken thermometers, evidence of the great importance attached to this code. Some scholars have argued that it was merely a method of limiting the number of offspring; but as it has been conclusively proved that the Roman Catholics produced more children on average than any other section of the community, this seems untenable. Other doctrines of the Roman Catholics included a belief in a Divine Redeemer and in a life after death.

Adam put the tray on the floor outside the bathroom, and entered purposefully. 'Come on, you're finished,' he said, lifting Clare from the seat.

'Wipe my bottom, please.'

He obliged, washing his hands afterwards to set a good example. Then he guided Clare firmly to the door.

'Can I stay and watch?'

'No. There's a biscuit for you on the kitchen table, and one each for Dominic and Edward.'

Adam micturated, and considered whether to wash his hands a second time. He decided against it. On re-entering the bedroom, he found Dominic urging his mother to rise.

'Up, up!' screamed the child. 'Dominic, leave your mother alone. She's busy,' said Adam. Burdened with the tray, he was too slow to prevent Dominic from pulling off the bedclothes. Barbara was the Callipygian type, but the thermometer spoiled the effect. Adam interposed himself between Dominic and the bed. 'Dominic, go away,' he said, and thoughtlessly remarked to Barbara: 'You look like a glass porcupine with all those things sticking out of you.'

Barbara yanked at the bedclothes and plucked the thermometer from her mouth. 'Don't be rude. Do you think I enjoy this performance every morning?'

'Well, yes, I do, as a matter of fact. It's like Camel and his pipe. You were both weaned too early. But this latest development . . . It strikes me as a bit kinky.'

'If you don't shut up, I'll break these damn things over my knee and –'

'Have a cup of tea,' said Adam conciliatingly.

'Just a minute.' Barbara entered the readings of her two

thermometers in a small Catholic diary. This was not a conscious irony on her part, but Adam followed the relationship between the liturgical year and his wife's temperature chart with interest. He practised a special devotion to those saints whose feast-days fell within the putative Safe Period, and experienced disquiet when a virgin martyr was so distinguished.

'Up, up!' shouted Dominic, red with anger.

'Dominic,' said Adam, 'Clare has got a bikky for you.'

The child trotted out. They sipped their tea.

'I wish you wouldn't use those silly baby-words, Adam.'

'Sorry. I keep forgetting. What was your temperature?' At this stage of Barbara's cycle, her temperature was of largely academic interest, except that marked changes from day to day might indicate that conception had taken place. Another cold wave of fear rippled through Adam's frame at the thought.

'One said 97.8 and the other 98.2.'

'What does this mean?'

'It's down a bit . . . I don't know.'

'Have you . . . You haven't started your period yet?' he asked wistfully.

'No. I don't think so.'

'Go and find out,' he wheedled.

'Give me a minute.'

How lovely it would be if she came back from the bathroom and said yes. How happy his day would be. How transfigured the British Museum would appear. With what zest he would collect his books and set to work . . . But he had forgotten to reserve any books. That meant a long delay this morning . . .

'Eh?' he said, conscious that Barbara had asked him a question.

'You haven't listened to a word I've been saying.'

'Yes I have,' he lied.

'What did I ask you, then?'

He groped around in his mind for a likely question. 'You said, why was I limping?'

'There, you see? I said, "Have you looked at Edward's rash?"'

'I didn't exactly look. But I don't remember noticing it.'

'I hope it isn't measles. Why *are* you limping anyway?'

'I don't know. I think I must have pulled a muscle.'

'What?'

'In the night.'

'Don't be ridiculous. How could you pull a muscle when you were asleep?'

'That's what I don't understand. Perhaps I run in my sleep.'

'Perhaps you do other things in your sleep,' said Barbara, getting out of bed and leaving the room.

Her words did not immediately sink into Adam's consciousness. He was fascinated by a mental picture of himself running through the streets of London in his pyjamas, at tremendous speed, chest out, arms pumping, mouth swallowing air, eyes glazed in sleep.

PYJAMA ATHLETE SMASHES RECORD

Early yesterday morning late-night revellers were astonished by the sight of a young man clad in pyjamas speeding through the streets of London. Herman Hopple, the British Olympic coach, spotted the mystery runner when returning to his Bloomsbury hotel, and having a stopwatch in his pocket, timed him at 1 minute 28.5 seconds as he lapped the British Museum before disappearing in the direction of Battersea. An official of the AAA who was fortunately accompanying Mr Hopple at the time later measured the perimeter of the British Museum at exactly 800 metres. The pyjama athlete has thus smashed the world record, and qualifies for the $10,000 prize established by an American millionaire for the first man to cover the distance in less than a minute and a half. 'We are very anxious to trace him,' said Mr Hopple this morning.

Barbara's words suddenly formed up and came resoundingly to attention in his mind. *Perhaps you do other things in your sleep.* Could you, he wondered, and not remember it? That would be the supreme irony: to conceive another child and not even be conscious enough to enjoy it. There was that night not long ago when they had come back from Camel's place drowsy and amorous from drinking Spanish wine . . .

Barbara returned from the bathroom, and shook her head at Adam's hopeful glance. She was carrying Edward under her arm, breech presentation.

'I've been thinking,' said Adam, 'about what you said just now. It's just possible you know. That evening we came back from Camel's. Do you remember, the next morning my pyjama trousers were on the floor and two buttons had come off your nightdress?'

'Don't be ridiculous,' said Barbara, rummaging in a drawer for a nappy. '*You* might not know what you were doing, but I would.'

'It's not ridiculous. What about *incubi* and *succubae*?'

'What about them?'

'They were demons who used to have intercourse with humans while they were asleep.'

'That's all I need,' said Barbara.

'How many days overdue are you?' Adam asked. As if he didn't know.

'Three.'

'Have you been that much before?'

'Yes.'

Barbara was bent over the wriggling torso of Edward, and her replies were muffled by the safety pins in her mouth. Barbara always seemed to have something in her mouth.

'Often?'

'No.'

'How often?'

'Oh, for God's sake, Adam!'

Barbara clicked the second pin shut, and let Edward slide to the floor. She looked up, and Adam saw with dismay that she was crying.

'What's the matter?' he wailed.

'I feel sick.'

Adam felt as if two giant hands had grasped his stomach and intestines, drenched them in cold water, and wrung them out like a dishcloth. 'Oh Jesus,' he murmured, employing the blasphemy he reserved for special occasions.

Barbara stared hopelessly at Edward, crawling across the lino. 'I can't think how we could have made a mistake. My temperature went up at the right time and everything.'

'Oh Jesus,' Adam repeated, aloud. When his own innate pessimism was balanced by Barbara's common sense, he could survive; but when Barbara herself was rattled, as she clearly was this morning, nothing could save him from falling deeper into despair. He could see it was going to be a bad day, of a kind he knew well. He would sit slumped at his desk in the British Museum, a heap of neglected books before him, while his mind reeled with menstrual cycles and temperature charts and financial calculations that never came right. He made a brief mental prayer: 'Please God, let her not be pregnant.' He added: 'And I'm sorry I swore.'

'Don't look at me like that,' said Barbara.

'Like what?'

'As if it was all my fault.'

'Of course it isn't your fault,' said Adam testily. 'Or mine either. But you don't expect to see the Lineaments of Gratified Desire all over my face, do you?'

The entrance of Clare and Dominic put an end to further conversation.

'Dominic says he's hungry,' Clare announced, accusingly.

*

'Why aren't you having any breakfast, Mummy?' asked Clare.

'Mummy doesn't feel well,' said Adam.

'Why don't you feel well, Mummy?'

'I don't know, Clare. I just feel sick.'

''ick,' said Dominic sociably.

'*I* only feel sick *after* I eat things,' observed Clare. 'So does Dominic, don't you Dominic?'

''ick.'

'*S*ick, Dominic. Say "*S*ick".'

''ick.'

'I wish to hell you wouldn't talk so much at breakfast, Clare,' Adam said.

'Don't lose your temper with the children, Adam,' Barbara intervened. 'Clare is only trying to teach Dominic.'

Adam swallowed the last morsel of his bacon without relish, and reached mechanically for the marmalade. Barbara intercepted him. 'Actually,' she said, 'I feel better now. I think I'll have some breakfast after all.'

Songbirds! A ray of sunshine! Bells ringing! Adam's heart lifted. Barbara smiled faintly at him and he raised his newspaper before his face to hide his absurd joy. An advertiser's announcement caught his eye:

> Write the second line of a rhyming couplet beginning:
> *I always choose a Brownlong chair.*
> ....
> – and win a new three-piece suite or £100 cash.

Now that was the kind of competition a literary man ought to be able to win. A modest prize, too, which should cut down the number of competitors to a reasonable size. *I always choose a Brownlong chair* ... Because ... because ... Ah! He had it. He read out the terms of the competition to his family.

' "*I always choose a Brownlong chair.*" What about the next line?'

'*Because it's made for wear and tear*,' suggested Clare.

'That's what I was going to say,' said Adam, resentfully.

When Adam came to dress, he could not find a pair of clean underpants. Barbara came into the room at this point, carrying Edward.

'I don't think he's got measles after all,' she said.

'Good. I can't find a pair of clean pants.'

'No, I washed them all yesterday. They're still damp.'

'Well, I'll just have to wear the pair I had on yesterday.' He moved towards the soiled linen basket.

'I washed those, too. While you were having your bath last night.'

Adam came to a halt, and rounded slowly on his wife. 'What are you telling me? D'you mean I haven't got a single pair of underpants to wear?'

'If you changed them more often, this wouldn't happen.'

'That may be so, but I'm not going to argue about personal hygiene at this point. What I want to know is: what am I going to wear under my trousers today?'

'Do you *have* to wear something? Can't you do without for once?'

'Of course I can't "do without"!'

'I don't know why you're making such a fuss. I've gone without pants before.' She looked meaningfully at Adam, who softened at the memory of a certain day by the sea.

'That was different. You know the trousers of my suit are itchy,' he complained in a quieter tone. 'You don't know what it's like, sitting in the Museum all day.'

'Wear your other trousers, then.'

'I've got to wear the suit today. There's a postgraduate sherry-party.'

'You didn't tell me.'

'Don't change the subject.'

13

Barbara was silent for a minute. 'You could wear a pair of mine,' she offered.

'To hell with that! What d'you take me for – a – transvestite? Where are those damp ones?'

'In the kitchen somewhere. They'll take a long time to dry.'

In the passage he nearly tripped over Clare, who was squatting on the floor, dressing a doll.

'What's a transvestite, Daddy?' she inquired.

'Ask your mother,' Adam snarled.

In the kitchen, Dominic was tearing the morning paper into narrow strips. Adam snatched it away from him, and the child began to scream. Cravenly, Adam returned the newspaper. He looked at the clock and began to get angry at the way time was slipping away. Time when he should be at work, work, work. Ploughing ahead with a thesis that would rock the scholarly world and start a revolution in literary criticism.

He found a pair of underpants in a tangle of sodden washing in the baby's bath. Improvising brilliantly, he pulled out the grill-pan of the electric stove, wiped the grid clean of grease with a handkerchief, and spread out his pants. He slotted home the grill-pan, and turned the switch to High. Fascinated, Dominic stopped tearing up the newspaper and watched the rising steam. Adam stealthily confiscated the remaining portion of the newspaper. The competition again caught his eye.

> I always choose a Brownlong chair
> Whenever I relax au pair.

Or

> I always choose a Brownlong chair
> For laying girls with long brown hair.

No, it was worth going in for seriously.

I always choose a Brownlong chair
For handsome looks and a price that's fair.

Didn't scan very well.

'Dadda, 'ire,' said Dominic, tugging gently at his sleeve. Adam smelled burning cloth, and lunged at the grill. Ire was the word. He stuffed the scorched remains of his underpants into the garbage pail, burning his fingers in the process.

'More, Dadda,' said Dominic.

In the passage Adam met Barbara. 'Where did you say your pants were?' he asked casually.

'In the top left-hand drawer.' She sniffed. 'You've burned something.'

'Nothing much,' he said, and hurried on to the bedroom.

Adam, who had hitherto valued women's underwear on its transparency, now found himself applying quite different standards, and deploring the frivolity of his wife's tastes. Eventually he located a pair of panties that were opaque, and a chaste white in hue. Unfortunately they were also trimmed with lace, but that couldn't be helped. As he drew them on, the hairs on his legs crackled with static electricity. The clinging but featherlight touch of the nylon round his haunches was a strange new sensation. He stood thoughtfully before the mirror for a moment, awed by a sudden insight into sexual deviation.

'Mummy says a transvestite is a poor man who likes wearing ladies' clothes because he's silly in the head,' remarked Clare from the door.

Adam grabbed his trousers and pulled them on. 'Clare, how many times have I told you not to come into this room without knocking. You're quite old enough to remember.'

'I didn't come in. I'm standing outside,' she replied, pointing to her feet.

'Don't answer back,' he said dispiritedly. What a mess he was making of his parental role this morning. Oh, it was going to be a bad day, all right.

Adam's family lined up in alphabetical order to be kissed goodbye: Barbara, Clare, Dominic and Edward (seated). When the principle behind this nomenclature dawned on their friends they were likely to ask humorously whether Adam and Barbara intended working through the whole alphabet, a joke that seemed less and less funny to Adam and Barbara as time went on. Adam kissed Barbara last, and scrutinized her for signs of pregnancy: coarse-grained skin, lifeless hair, swelling breasts. He even looked at her waistline. With an immense effort of rationality, he reminded himself that she was only three days overdue.

'How do you feel?'

'Oh, all right. We must try and be sensible.'

'I don't know what we'll do if you're pr –'

'*Pas devant les enfants.*'

'Eh?'

'That means, not in front of us,' Clare explained to Dominic.

'Oh yes,' said Adam, catching on. 'I'll phone you later.'

'Try and do it when Mrs Green is out.'

Dominic began to snivel. 'Where Dadda going?' he demanded.

'He's going to work, like he always does,' said Barbara.

'At the British Museum,' Adam said impressively. As he closed the door of the flat, he heard Clare asking Barbara if there were any other transvestites at the British Museum.

2

As I go to my work at the British Museum I see the faces of the people become daily more corrupt.

Ruskin

When the door of the Applebys' flat was closed, the staircase leading to the ground floor was plunged in total darkness, as the single switch of the hall light was at the bottom, near the telephone, and was always kept in the 'off' position by Mrs Green. Adam groped for the banister, and slowly descended the stairs, impeded by the two canvas holdalls he carried, one containing books and the other papers; having discovered with tiresome frequency that whatever portion of his thesis material he left at home he was bound to need at the British Museum, he had resigned himself to carrying the whole apparatus backwards and forwards every day.

He was making good progress down the stairs when his cautiously extended foot encountered a soft, yielding, object. He drew back his foot with a gasp of fright. He stared hard, but could distinguish nothing in the gloom.

'Pussy?' he murmured. But if it was Mrs Green's cat, it was asleep – or dead. The foot he inched forward again aroused no life in the mysterious object.

The thing to do, of course, was to step smartly over it, whistling loudly. But somehow the idea was distasteful. He recalled a novel he had read about a man who had been locked up by the Gestapo in total darkness with a sinister, soft, moist, yielding object, which the man in his terror imagined to be all kinds of horrible things, such as a piece of human flesh looking like a lump of raw meat, but which turned out to be nothing more than a wet cloth. Adam placed his bags on the stairs behind him, and struck a match. It was a lump of raw meat.

'Is that you, Mr Appleby?' inquired Mrs Green, as Adam's half-stifled scream lingered in the air. The light came on in the hall.

'Is this yours?' inquired Adam, with cold politeness, indicating the cellophane-wrapped joint at his feet. Mrs Green came to the foot of the stairs and looked up.

'Mrs Appleby asked me to get it for her. I was out shopping early this morning.' She bounced a reproachful look at Adam off the dial of the clock in the hall. Mrs Green considered it little less than criminal for a married man with three children to be leaving the house in the middle of the morning, and not to work either, but just to sit in a library reading books. Her look, however, accused him of more than idleness. Adam knew very well what Mrs Green supposed him to have been up to, while respectable people had been up and about.

To Mrs Green, herself a widow with an only son, Adam's paternity of three young children, whom he could patently not afford to support, indicated an ungovernable sexual appetite of which Barbara was the innocent victim. 'Ooh, isn't Mr Appleby naughty?' had been her first response to Barbara's nervous announcement of her third pregnancy; and subsequently Adam had had to endure from his landlady the kind of half-fascinated, half-fearful appraisal usually reserved for prize bulls. As he calculated that there could be few married men in Metropolitan London who enjoyed their marital rights as seldom as himself, he found this situation particularly trying. But it was difficult to communicate to Mrs Green the true state of affairs. Shortly after Edward had been born she had taken Barbara aside, and hinted that there were Things You Could Use, and that she had heard it rumoured that there were Clinics where they gave you the Things, not that she had any experience of them herself, she had never been troubled that way with poor Mr G., he was more for the fretwork, but she thought she owed it to Mrs Appleby to tell her. Barbara had thanked her and explained that their religious convictions prevented them from profiting by her advice. Undeterred, Mrs Green had consulted a female relative who belonged to some obscure non-conformist sect, and returned with the counsel, 'You'll just have to Pull Away, dear, at the critical moment, if you get my meaning; just Pull Away.' Adam and Barbara tolerated these intrusions into their private lives for the sake of the flat, the rent of which Mrs Green had not raised during their tenancy out of compassion for Barbara.

'I hope you haven't hurt that meat, Mr Appleby,' Mrs Green remarked as Adam reached the hall. 'I see you're limping.'

'No, no, the meat's quite all right,' Adam replied. 'My leg's been hurting since I got up. I think I must have pulled a muscle.'

'You ought to get more exercise,' said Mrs Green, adding meaningfully, 'in the open air. It's not healthy to be reading all day.'

'Well, I won't get much reading done today unless I hurry,' he replied jovially, bustling to the door. 'Good-bye.'

'Oh, Mr Appleby –'

He got the door swinging just in time to pretend that he hadn't heard, but in the instant before it slammed behind him he caught the end of her sentence:

'– a letter for you.'

A letter. Adam experienced a kind of psychic salivation at the thought of a letter waiting for him behind the door. He loved mail, even though his own consisted almost exclusively of bills, rejected scholarly articles and appeals for donations from missionary nuns who obtained his address from letters he wrote to the Catholic press about Birth Control. He had a tantalizing mental image of the letter on Mrs Green's hallstand – he could swear now that he had seen it out of the corner of his eye as he had rushed for the door – not a bill, not an appeal, not a creased brown foolscap envelope addressed in his own handwriting, but a plump letter in a thick, white, expensive envelope, his name and address typed on it in a distinctive typeface, a crest on the flap suggestive of an important, semi-official source, a letter bringing good fortune: *Would you accept . . . We should like to commission . . . It is my pleasure to inform you . . . State your own terms . . .*

He would have to concede that he had heard Mrs Green's parting words, and return ignominiously. With luck, she would already have retreated to the kitchen which, appropriately enough, always reeked with the smell of cooking cabbage. Adam fumbled in his pocket for his keys, only to discover that he had left them in the flat. He agitated the door-knocker gently and apologetically. There was no sound from within. He knocked harder. Stooping, he pushed open the flap of the letter-box, and called coaxingly, 'Mrs Green!' To his surprise an envelope flew out of the aperture and lodged itself between his teeth.

'Thank you, Mrs Green,' he called, spitting out the missive, and glaring at a small boy who was sniggering on the pavement.

The appearance of the letter was as odd as the manner of its delivery. The envelope was a specimen of old-fashioned mourning stationery, with a thick black band round the edges. It appeared to have been formerly used in correspondence with a restaurateur, but wrongly addressed, so that it bore much evidence of the patient efforts of the GPO to deliver it correctly. The envelope was sealed with Elastoplast, and Adam's name and address trailed between the other cancelled addresses in heavy green biro. Exerting all his palaeographic skills, Adam made out at the primary level of the palimpsest the name, 'Mrs Amy Rottingdean', who, he deduced, was the probable source of the letter addressed to himself. He was unable to attach the name to anyone he knew. Scrutinizing the envelope, Adam quivered slightly with expectancy and curiosity. He found the sensation pleasant, and to prolong it thrust the letter into his pocket. Then he braced himself to confront his scooter.

Adam kept his scooter under a filthy tarpaulin in Mrs Green's small front garden. He pulled off the tarpaulin, kicked it under the hedge, and regarded the machine with loathing. He had been given the scooter by its former owner, his father-in-law, when the latter's firm had provided him with a small car. At the time, he had regarded the gift as one of astounding generosity, but he was now convinced that it had been an act of the purest malice, designed either to maim him or ruin him, or both. He had accepted the gift on the assumption that the running costs would be more than compensated for by the savings on fares, a prediction that still wrung from him a bitter laugh whenever he recalled it, which was usually when he was paying for repairs. Paying for repairs was, however, one of Adam's smaller worries. *Getting* the damned thing repaired was infinitely more difficult.

Of all the industries in the country, Adam had decided, scooter-maintenance exhibited the most sensational excess of demand over supply. In theory, a fortune awaited the man who set out to meet this demand; but at the bottom of his heart Adam doubted whether scooters were repairable in the ordinary sense of the term: they were the butterflies of the road, fragile organisms which took a long time to make and a short time to die. By now, Adam had located every workshop within a five-mile radius of his flat, and without exception they were crammed to the ceiling with crippled scooters waiting for repair. In a small clearing in the middle of the floor, a few oily youths would be tinkering doubtfully with a dismantled machine or two, while their owners, and the owners of other machines in dock, loitered anxiously outside trying to catch the eyes of the mechanics to bribe them with cigarettes or money. Adam, an innocent in the world of machinery at the best of times, had experienced the most humiliating and desperate moments of his life in scooter-repair workshops.

Adam strapped his heavy bags to the luggage rack, and pushed the scooter into the road. He gave the starting pedal a ritual kick, and was so astonished when the engine fired that he was too slow in twisting the throttle. The engine died, and a dozen further kicks produced not the faintest symptom of internal combustion. Adam resigned himself to adopting his normal procedure for starting the motor. Grasping the handlebars firmly, he selected second gear, disengaged the clutch, and pushed the scooter along the road with increasing momentum. When he had attained the speed of a brisk trot, he abruptly let out the clutch. A juddering shock was transmitted from the engine, via the handlebars, to his arms and shoulders. The engine wheezed and coughed, inexorably reducing Adam's speed. Just as he had abandoned hope, the engine fired and the scooter leapt forward at full throttle, dragging Adam with it. With feet flying and duffle-coat flapping, Adam careered past interested housewives and cheering children for some fifty yards before he recovered sufficient balance to scramble on to the seat. His pulled muscle throbbed painfully from the exertion. Reducing speed, he chugged off in the direction of the Albert Bridge.

A notice at the approach to this bridge undermined confidence in its structure by requesting soldiers to break step while marching over it. Adam foresaw the time when he would be the innocent victim of military vanity.

– The men seem in good spirit this morning, Ponsonby.
– Yes, sir.
– Keeping step very well.
– Yes, sir. Sir, we're approaching the Albert Bridge.
– Are we, Ponsonby? Remind me to compliment Sar'nt Major on the men's marching, will you?

– Yes, sir. About the Albert Bridge, sir – shall I give the order to break step?

– Break step, Ponsonby? What are you talking about?

– Well, there's a notice, sir, which requests soldiers to break step while marching over the bridge. I suppose it sets up vibrations . . .

– Vibrations, Ponsonby? Never let it be said that the 41st was afraid of vibrations.

– Sir, if I might –

– No, Ponsonby. I'm afraid this is a blatant example of the civil power's encroachment on military territory.

– But sir, we're already on the bridge –

– Ponsonby!

– Safety of other people, sir!

– There's only some long-haired layabout on one of those silly scooter things. March on, Ponsonby, march on!

And so the column of soldiers would march proudly on over the bridge, feet drumming on the tarmac. The bridge would quiver and shake, wires twang, girders snap, the road subside, and the soldiers step nonchalantly over the brink, as he himself was hurled into the cold Thames, with only a faint plume of steam to mark the spot where he and his scooter had disappeared beneath the surface.

Lost in this reverie, Adam drifted towards a huge limousine halted at traffic lights, and pulled up just in time. The advertising copy for this model, he recalled, drew particular attention to the fact that the blades of the fan which cooled the radiator were *irregularly set* to reduce noise. It had been news to Adam that the fan caused noise: certainly it was not detectable on his own machine beneath the din of the exhaust and the rattling of various insecurely attached parts of the bodywork.

Inside the limousine, a fat man was smoking a fat cigar and dictating into a portable dictaphone. Adam turned in his saddle to face a melancholy line of people queueing for a bus.

'O tempora, O mores!' he declaimed, his voice rendered safely inaudible by the noise of his machine.

A man stepped forward from the queue and approached Adam, evidently under the impression that he had been personally addressed. Adam recognized him as Father Finbar Flannegan, a curate of his own parish, whom he and Barbara, in a private opinion poll, had voted Priest Most Likely to Prevent the Conversion of England.

'It's very kind of you to offer me a lift, Mr Appleby,' said Father Finbar, climbing on to the pillion. 'Could you drop me off near Westminster Cathedral?'

'Have you ever been a pillion passenger before, Father?' asked Adam, doubtfully.

'I have not, Mr Appleby,' replied the priest. 'But I'm sure you're a very capable driver. Besides, I'm late for my conference.'

'What conference is that, Father?' inquired Adam, moving off with the limousine, as the lights changed.

'Oh, it's some Monsignor or other who's giving a lecture on the Council to the priests of the diocese. One priest was invited from each parish, so we tossed up for it, and I lost.'

Adam heeled over the scooter to turn right, and his passenger tried to compensate by leaning in the opposite direction, yachtsman-style. The machine wobbled perilously, and Adam found himself clasped in a painful embrace by the alarmed priest who, he observed in the wing-mirror, had pulled his black Homburg down over his ears to leave his hands free.

'It's easier if you lean over with me,' observed Adam.

'Don't you worry, Mr Appleby. I have my Saint Christopher medal with me, thanks be to God.'

These, and subsequent remarks, had to be shouted to be audible above the din of the scooter and the background traffic noise.

It did not surprise Adam that Father Finbar lacked enthusiasm for the Second Vatican Council, on which he and Barbara and most of their Catholic friends pinned their hopes for a humane and liberal life in the Church. Father Finbar's ideas about the Catholic Faith were very much formed by his upbringing in Tipperary, and he seemed to regard the London parish in which he worked as a piece of the Old Country which had broken off in a storm and floated across the sea until it lodged itself in the Thames Basin. The parish was indeed at least half-populated by Irish, but this was not, in Adam and Barbara's eyes, an adequate excuse for nostalgic allusions to 'Back Home' in sermons, or the sanctioning of collections in the church porch for the dependants of IRA prisoners. As to the liturgical reform and the education of the laity, Father Finbar's rosary beads rattled indignantly in his pocket at the very mention of such schemes, and he would, Adam suspected, chain up all the missals in the parish at the drop of a biretta.

Indignation rising in his breast at these thoughts, Adam coaxed his scooter above the statutory speed limit, and embarked upon some stylish traffic-weaving. He even managed to overtake the limousine, in which the fat man with the fat cigar was now using a radio telephone. In his right ear, he heard the Litany of Our Lady being recited in a tone of increasing panic.

The wind whistled through the rents in his windshield, and made Adam's eyes water. But he always enjoyed his morning sprint along the Embankment. The Thames lay folded in fog; but away from the river the fog cleared, and the orange disc of the sun was clearly visible. A turn in the road brought into view the campanile of Westminster Cathedral, the most blatantly phallic shape on the London skyline.

The spectacle and the association deflected Adam's thoughts into a familiar channel, and he waxed melancholy at the recollection of Barbara's symptoms that morning. He grew convinced that they had had intercourse while sleeping off the effect of Camel's Spanish wine, and he tried unsuccessfully to work out the position of that evening in Barbara's current cycle.

He released his grip on the handlebars to count with his fingers, but his passenger, abandoning prayer, shrieked a protest into his ear.

'For the love of God, Mr Appleby, will you take a little care!'

'Sorry, Father,' said Adam. Then, on a sudden impulse, he yelled back over his shoulder, 'Do you think the Council will change the Church's attitude on Birth Control?'

'What was that, Mr Appleby?'

Adam repeated his question at louder volume, and the scooter lurched as his passenger registered its import.

'The Church's teaching never changes, Mr Appleby,' came the stiff reply. 'On that or any other matter.'

A traffic jam blocked the road ahead, and Adam went down through the gears to save his ailing brakes. Father Finbar's teeth chattered under the stress of vibration.

'Well, all right – let's say "develop",' Adam went on. 'Newman's theory of doctrinal development –'

'Newman?' interjected the priest sharply. 'Wasn't he a Protestant?'

'Circumstances have changed, new methods are available – isn't it time we revised our thinking about these matters?'

'Mr Appleby, I don't have to explain to a man of your education the meaning of the Natural Law . . .'

'Oh, but excuse me Father, that's just what you do have to explain. Modern continental theologians are questioning the whole –'

'Don't talk to me about thim German and French!' exclaimed Father Finbar furiously. 'They're worse than the Protestants themselves. They're deshtroying the Church, leading the Faithful astray. Why, half the parish is straining at the leash already. One hint from the Pope and they'd be off on a wild debauch.'

'You mean, fulfilling the true purpose of marriage!' protested Adam.

'The true purpose of marriage is to procreate children and

26

bring them up in the fear and love of God!' asserted Father Finbar.

Adam, his scooter locked in traffic, twisted in his saddle. 'Look, Father, the average woman marries at twenty-three and is fertile till forty. Is it her duty to procreate seventeen children?'

'I was the youngest of eighteen children!' cried the priest triumphantly.

'How many survived infancy?' demanded Adam.

'Seven,' the priest admitted. 'God rest the souls of the others.' He crossed himself.

'You see? With modern medical care they might all survive. But how could you house and feed even seven in London today? What are we supposed to do?'

'Practice self-restraint,' retorted the priest. '*I do.*'

'That's different –'

'Pray, go to daily communion, say the rosary together . . .'

'We can't. We're too busy –'

He was going to say: 'changing bloody nappies'; but became aware that a strange silence had fallen upon the traffic, and that his dialogue with Father Finbar was being listened to with interested attention by the bystanders and drivers leaning out of their cars.

'We must talk about it again, Father,' he said wearily. In a curious way, the discussion had made Father Finbar more human, and Adam felt he would not be able to invoke him so easily in future as a symbol of blind ecclesiastical reaction.

The strange silence was explained by the fact that most of the drivers around him, evidently resigned to a long wait, had switched off their engines. Adam now followed suit.

'What's going on?' he wondered aloud.

'I think a policeman is holding up the traffic,' said Father Finbar, dismounting. 'If you don't mind, Mr Appleby, I think I'll walk from here. Perhaps the Queen is driving through.'

'OK, Father. You'll get there quicker on foot.'

'Thank you for the lift, Mr Appleby. And for the discussion. You should join the Legion of Mary.'

His black Homburg hat still pulled down over his ears, Father Finbar threaded his way through the stationary vehicles, and pushed through the bystanders lining the pavement.

An expectant hush had fallen on the scene. From near-by Westminster, Mrs Dalloway's clock boomed out the half hour. It partook, he thought, shifting his weight in the saddle, of metempsychosis, the way his humble life fell into moulds prepared by literature. Or was it, he wondered, picking his nose, the result of closely studying the sentence structure of the English novelists? One had resigned oneself to having no private language any more, but one had clung wistfully to the illusion of a personal property of events. A fond and fruitless illusion, it seemed, for here, inevitably, came the limousine, with its Very Important Personage, or Personages, dimly visible in the interior. The policeman saluted, and the crowd pressed forward, murmuring, 'Philip', 'Tony and Margaret', 'Prince Andrew'.

Then a huge plosive shout of 'The Beatles!' went up, and the crowd suddenly became very young and disorderly. Engines revved, horns blared, drivers cursed, and the wedge of traffic inched its way forward through the herds of screaming, weeping teenagers who spilled out into the road and pursued the vanishing car. A familiar figure in black darted in front of Adam, and he braked sharply.

'Did you see them, Mr Appleby? It's the Beatles!' cried Father Finbar, red with excitement. 'One of them's a Catholic, you know.' He lumbered off after the other fans.

Only one figure kept a still repose in the ebb and flow of vehicles and people. At the edge of the pavement an old, old lady, white-haired and wrinkled, dressed in sober black and elastic-sided boots, stood nobly erect, as if she thought some-one really important had passed. In her right hand she held a speaking trumpet, which she raised to her ear. Adam, drawing level with her as the traffic surged slowly forward, murmured 'Clarissa!' and the old lady looked at him sharply. Suddenly frightened, Adam accelerated and drove off recklessly in the direction of Bloomsbury. Bloomsbury. *Bloomsbury!*

3

I have seen all sorts of domes of Peters and Pauls, Sophia, Pantheon
– what not? – and have been struck by none of them as much as by
that catholic dome in Bloomsbury, under which our million volumes
are housed. What peace, what love, what truth, what happiness for
all, what generous kindness for you and for me are here spread out!
It seems to me one cannot sit down in that place without a heart full
of grateful reverence. I own to have said my grace at the table, and
to have thanked Heaven for this my English birthright, freely to
partake of these bountiful books and speak the truth I find there.

Thackeray

Adam drove noisily down Great Russell Street and, bouncing in
the saddle, swerved through the gates of the British Museum.
He took some minutes finding a space into which he could
squeeze his scooter: many businessmen had discovered that by
leaving their cars in the South forecourt, walking through the
Museum and sneaking out through the North Door, they could
enjoy free parking all day in the centre of London.

He limped slowly towards the colossal portico, balancing the
weight of his two holdalls. The Museum wore an autumnal
aspect, as if built of petrified fog. The gilt statuary reclining
above the bulging pillars provided the only gleam of colour.
Pigeons stalked grumpily about, ruffling their feathers as if they
felt the cold. Tourists were sparse. The British Museum was
returning to its winter role – refuge for scholars, postgraduates
and other bums and layabouts in search of a warm seat. In

particular, Adam regretted the departure of the pretty girls who sat on the steps in summer, eating sandwiches and writing postcards, their carelessly disposed legs providing an alluring spectacle for men approaching on ground level.

It seemed base, somehow, to come daily to this great temple of learning, history and artistic achievement in the same weary, mechanical spirit as the jaded clerk to his city office. But there it was: not even the British Museum was proof against the sedation of routine. Adam pushed listlessly at the revolving doors and crossed the main hall with dogged, unswerving steps. As always, he vowed that one day he would really go and look at the Elgin Marbles, which could be glimpsed to his left, but the vow carried no conviction. The previous year, he and Camel had drawn up an elaborate plan for acquainting themselves with the whole Museum by inspecting one gallery a day in their lunch hour. If he remembered rightly, they had given up after looking at only Japanese armour and Egyptian vases.

There was one feature of his diurnal pilgrimage to the British Museum that afforded Adam a modest but constant gratification, and that was the fact that, as a familiar figure, he was not asked to show his card on entering the Reading Room. When he passed the doorkeeper with just a nod of greeting he assumed, he hoped, an air of importance for the group of casual visitors who invariably hung about outside the door, trying to peer into the Reading Room.

'Could I see your card, sir?'

Adam, his hand already on the swing door, halted and looked with astonishment and hurt pride at the doorkeeper, who grinned and pointed to a notice requesting all readers to show their cards that day.

'The annual check, sir,' he said, taking Adam's card from his hand. 'Ah, two months out of date. I'm afraid you'll have to go and renew it.'

'Oh look, I'm late as it is this morning. Can't I do it after I've ordered my books?'

'Sorry, sir.'

Adam dropped his bags with an angry thud at the feet of an Easter Island god, and stumped off to renew the ticket. Near the Elgin Marbles was a heavy door, guarded by a stern-looking porter with a huge key. When notified of Adam's errand, this official grudgingly unlocked the door, and ushered him into a long corridor. He then rang a little bell, and went out again, *locking the door behind him*.

Adam, or A as he would now more vaguely have identified himself, had been all through this before, but could not be sure whether he had dreamed it or actually experienced it. He was trapped. Behind him was a locked, guarded door; in front of him a long corridor terminating in a room. He could not go back. He could not stay where he was – the men in the room at the end of the corridor, warned by the bell, were expecting him. He went reluctantly forward, down the long corridor, between the smooth polished wooden cabinets, locked and inscrutable, which formed the walls, stretching high out of reach. Craning his neck to see if they reached the high ceiling, A felt suddenly dizzy, and leaned against the wall for support.

The room at the end of the corridor was an office, with a long, curving counter behind which sat two men, neat, self-possessed, expectant. A approached the nearer man, who immediately began writing on a piece of paper.

'Yes?' he said, after a few minutes had passed, and without looking up.

A, his mouth unaccountably dry, enunciated with difficulty the words, 'Reading Room ticket'.

'Over there.'

A sidled along the counter to the second man, who immediately began writing in a ledger. A waited patiently.

'Yes?' said the second man, closing his ledger with a snap that made A jump.

'IwanttorenewmyReadingRoomticket,' gabbled A.

'Over there.'

'But I've just been over there. He sent me to you.' Out of the corner of his eye, A saw the first man watching them intently.

The second man scrutinized him for what seemed a very long time, then spoke. 'One moment.' He went over to the first man, and they held a whispered conference, at the conclusion of which the first man came over to A and sat down in the second man's seat.

'What is it you want, exactly?' he asked.

'I want to renew my Reading Room ticket,' said A patiently.

'You want to *renew* it? You mean you have a ticket already?'

'Yes.'

'May I see it?'

A presented his ticket.

'It's out of date,' observed the man.

'That's why I want to renew it!' A exclaimed.

'When did you last use the Reading Room?'

'Two months ago,' lied A, cunningly.

'You haven't used it since your ticket expired?'

'No.'

'It wouldn't matter if you had,' said the man. 'As long as you're not lying.' He tore A's ticket neatly into four sections, and deposited them in a waste-paper basket. It distressed A to see his ticket torn up. He experienced a queasy, empty feeling in his stomach.

'So now you want to renew your annual ticket?'

'Please.'

'You see, you didn't make that clear to me just now.'

'I'm sorry.'

'I assumed you were a casual reader wanting a short-term ticket. That's why I sent you to my colleague.' He nodded in the direction of the second man. 'But when he realized you wanted an annual ticket, he directed you back to me. That is the reason for our apparently contradictory behaviour.'

He flashed a sudden smile, displaying a row of gold-filled teeth.

'I see. I'm afraid it was my fault,' A apologized.

'Don't mention it,' said the first man, opening the ledger and beginning to write.

'Could I have my new ticket now?' said A, after some minutes had passed.

'Over there.'

'But you just said you were responsible for renewing annual tickets!' protested A.

'Ah, but that was when I was sitting over there,' said the first man. 'We've changed places now. We do that from time to time. So that if one of us should fall ill,' he continued, 'the other can cover his work.'

A made his way wearily to the second man.

'Good morning. Can I help you?' said the second man, as if greeting him for the first time.

'I want to renew my annual Reading Room ticket,' said A.

'Certainly. May I see your old ticket?'

'No, the other man – gentleman – has just torn it up.'

'It *was* an annual ticket you had?'

'Yes. He just tore it up. Didn't you see him?'

The second man shook his head gravely. 'This is very irregular. You shouldn't have given him the ticket. He's on short-term tickets now.'

'Look, all I want is to have my ticket renewed. What does it matter which of you does it?'

'I'm afraid I can't renew a ticket which, as far as I'm concerned, doesn't exist.'

A gripped the counter tightly and closed his eyes. 'What do you suggest I do then?' he whispered hoarsely.

'I could give you a short-term ticket . . .'

'No that won't do. I'm working here every day. My livelihood depends upon my being here every day.'

'Then I can only suggest that you come back when my

colleague and I have changed places again,' said the second man.

'When will that be?'

'Oh there's no telling. You can wait if you like . . . in that room over there . . . you'll find plenty of people to chat to while you're waiting . . . your name will be called . . .'

'Are you all right, sir?'

Adam found himself lying on the floor of the corridor. The doorkeeper and some other people were bending over him with looks of concern. Scattered over the blood beside him were fragments of his expired Reading Room ticket. He rose unsteadily to his feet. His head ached.

'What happened? Did I faint?'

'Looks like it, sir. Would you like to lie down somewhere?'

'No thanks. I'm all right. If I could just get my Reading Room ticket renewed . . .'

'This way, sir.'

As he stooped to reclaim his bags, which lay, like votive offerings, at the feet of the pagan god, Adam felt his shoulder clasped in a bony grip.

'And what sort of a time is *this*, Appleby, to get into the Museum?'

Adam straightened up and turned.

'Oh, hallo Camel. I got held up by the Beatles. I think they were on their way to open Parliament.'

'Don't give me any excuses,' continued Camel in his hectoring voice. 'Do you realize that there are droves of eager industrious scholars prowling round the Reading Room in search of a seat, while the one I illegally saved for you –'

'I hope it's a padded one.'

'It is indeed a padded one, which only adds to the offence . . . Come and have a smoke,' he concluded, losing the thread of his sentence.

Adam had given up smoking when Dominic was born but, always eager for distraction, he usually accompanied Camel during the latter's periodic consumption of nicotine in the Museum colonnade. Conscience pricked him now more sharply than usual.

'Oh look, Camel, not today. I must get on.'

'Nonsense, old boy,' said Camel, in his bland tempter's voice, steering the willing Adam towards the exit. 'You look tired, peaky. A breath of air will do you the world of good. Besides, I've just thought of some new legislation that I want to tell you about.'

'Oh, all right, just for a minute.'

'You may entertain that pretence if you wish,' said Camel sardonically, now sure of Adam's company.

'It's too cold out here,' complained Adam, as they emerged into the raw, damp air. 'Why don't we have a coffee in the cafeteria instead?'

'I detest the cafeteria, as you well know. The Museum has degenerated since the cafeteria was introduced. When *I* started my research, we had no such luxuries. There was nowhere to go for a smoke – nowhere, mark you, in the entire building. You had to go out on to the colonnade, even in the bitterest weather. We had several cases of frostbite. I remember,' he went on, in his old soldier's voice, 'in the winter of '57 . . . Scholars brought back frozen stiff, pipe-stems bitten through. Had to thaw 'em out in the North Library. You youngsters have no idea.'

Camel (whose surname fitted so perfectly his long, stiff-legged stride, humped shoulders and droll, thick-lipped countenance, that it was generally taken to be an inspired nickname) did not seem to be particularly old, but he had been doing his Ph.D. thesis as long as anyone could remember. Its title – 'Sanitation in Victorian Fiction' – seemed modest enough; but, as Camel would patiently explain, the absence of references to sanitation was as significant as the presence of the same, and his work thus embraced the entire corpus of Victorian fiction. Further, the Victorian period was best understood as a period of transition in which the comic treatment of human excretion in the eighteenth century was suppressed, or sublimated in terms of social reform, until it re-emerged as a source of literary symbolism in the work of Joyce and other moderns. Camel's preparatory reading spread out in wider and wider circles, and it often seemed that he was bent on exhausting the entire resources of the Museum library before commencing composition. Some time ago a wild rumour had swept through Bloomsbury to the effect that Camel had written his first chapter, on the hygiene of Neanderthal Man; but Camel had wistfully denied it. 'I'm the modern Casaubon,' he would say. 'Don't expect progress.' He had no Dorothea to support, however, and earned enough by teaching evening classes in English to foreign students to keep himself.

'Well, what's your new legislation, then?' Adam inquired, as they seated themselves on a grimy wooden bench, flecked with pigeon droppings, at the extremity of one wing of the colonnade. He and Camel had devised a game, now of long standing, entitled, 'When We Are In Power'. This consisted in their imagining themselves to enjoy absolute political power, and thus the freedom to impose any law they liked upon the community – an opportunity which they would exploit not for the purposes of any crude self-advantage, nor to promote a programme of large-scale and idealistic reform but merely to iron out the smaller inequalities of life, overlooked by the professional legislators, and to score off sections of the populace against whom they had a grudge, such as taxi-drivers, generals and scooter-manufacturers.

'Well, I've been thinking,' said Camel, plugging his pipe with tobacco, 'that it's time we turned our attention to the private motorist. Now what would you say is the greatest injustice in that area?'

'They have cars, and we haven't.'

'Yes, of course. But When We Are In Power, we shall have cars ourselves. But you're on the right track. Has it occurred to you why so many people, of no apparent distinction in life, are able to run cars? And not just old, wheezing, corroding, bald-tyred, unreliable vehicles such as you or I may, with luck, look forward to owning after many years of labour, but shiny, new, powerful models straight out of the showroom?'

Adam thought for a moment, and remembered his father-in-law.

'Because they got them from their firms?'

'Right. Now –'

'You want to abolish firms' cars?'

'No, no. That's much too crude. You're losing your finesse, Appleby. We must keep within the bounds of possibility.'

'You could prohibit the use of business cars for pleasure.'

'Too difficult to enforce, though I did consider it for a while. No, what I hit upon was this: All cars supplied by commercial firms, government authorities or other institutions, must have painted on them, on both sides, the name of the firm, authority or other institution, together with the appropriate trade mark, symbol, coat-of-arms or iconic representation of the product.'

'Marvellous,' said Adam.

'I thought you'd like it,' said Camel, with shy pride.

'It's a classic. It's founded on a simple desire for truth. No one can object.'

'But how they'll hate it! Just imagine any suburban street after the law is passed,' said Camel, gloatingly. 'All those sleek new cars with "Jeyes Fluid" or "Heinz 57 Varieties" plastered all over them.'

Adam giggled. 'My father-in-law travels in fertilizer.' He added anxiously: 'Shouldn't we specify a minimum size for the lettering?'

'A good point. Six inches, would you say?'

'Nine.'

'Nine.'

They sat, sniggering quietly to themselves, for several minutes.

'You're looking better,' said Camel, at length. 'You did look queer just now.'

'I had a queer experience,' said Adam, deciding to confide in Camel. '. . . And this morning on my way to the Museum,' he concluded, 'I met Mrs Dalloway grown into an old woman.'

Camel regarded him with concern.

'I say, you want to watch this, you know. Are you over-working?'

Adam uttered a hollow laugh. 'Does it look like it?'

'Something else worrying you, then?'

'Something else is always worrying me.'

'Barbara's not pregnant again?'

'God, I hope not; but she felt sick this morning.'

'Ah,' said Camel.

As they re-entered the Museum, Adam asked Camel casually, 'By the way, what date was it that we came round to you?'

Camel consulted his diary. 'The 13th. Why?'

'Oh, nothing. You must come round to us soon. Look, I'm just going to ring Barbara. Don't wait.'

'You know Appleby, I don't think you're going to get as far as the Reading Room today.'

'I won't be a moment.'

To Adam's annoyance, Mrs Green answered the phone.

'Oh, hallo Mrs Green. Could I speak to Barbara, please?'

'Is that you, Mr Appleby? Did you get your letter?'

Adam had completely forgotten the letter. He patted his pocket. It was still there.

'Yes, I did, Mrs Green, thank you. Is Barbara there?'

'I'll call up the stairs.'

While he was waiting for Barbara, Adam took out the letter and inspected it with renewed curiosity. He was trying to open it with one hand, when Barbara picked up the phone.

'Hallo, Adam?'

'Hallo, darling,' said Adam, thrusting the letter back into his pocket. 'How are you feeling?'

'Oh, all right.'

'No queasiness?'

'No. Only a little.'

'You *do* feel queasy, then?'

'Only a little. Look, Adam –'

'Camel says we had those drinks with him on the 13th. Where does that come in the temperature chart?'

'Look, Adam, I can't discuss that now.'

'Why not?'

'I just can't. And it's absurd anyway.'

'You mean Mrs Green is listening?'

'Of course.'

'All right. I'll ring back later. But just check on the 13th, will you?'

'No, I won't.'

'How are the children?' Adam asked, pretending he hadn't heard.

'What do you mean? How are the children? You saw them less than two hours ago.'

'It seems longer than that.'

'Adam, are you feeling all right?'

'I'm fine. I'll ring back. Oh, I had a letter today.'

'Who from?'

'I don't know.'

'Adam, you're not all right.'

'Yes I am. I haven't had time to open it. It's been a terrible morning. I'll ring back.'

'Adam –'

''Bye, darling.' Adam put down the phone, and took the letter out of his pocket. Someone tapped on the window of the telephone kiosk. It was the fat man with the fat cigar he

40

had seen in the limousine. Adam opened the door.

'If you've finished in there,' said the fat man, waving his cigar, 'I have an urgent call to make.' He spoke with an American accent.

'Yes, I've finished,' said Adam, emerging from the kiosk. 'If you don't mind my pointing it out, you're not allowed to smoke inside the Museum.'

'Is that so? Thanks for the tip. Do you have any small change?'

'How much do you want?' said Adam.

'I want to call Denver, Colorado.'

'Not that much,' said Adam. 'You'd need about sixty shillings. Or a hundred and twenty sixpences. Or . . . two hundred and forty threepenny bits. There's a bank round the corner,' he concluded.

'You should be president of it, young man,' said the fat American. 'Take my accountant's adding machine away and he wouldn't know how many fingers he had.'

'Yes, well . . . if you want to use the phone.' Adam gestured politely to the empty booth. 'Perhaps you could reverse the charges.'

'Collect? That's a good idea. You're a great nation,' said the fat man, as he squeezed himself into the booth.

Adam muttered a farewell, and hastened to the Reading Room, brandishing his new ticket in readiness.

He passed through the narrow vaginal passage, and entered the huge womb of the Reading Room. Across the floor, dispersed along the radiating desks, scholars curled, foetus-like, over their books, little buds of intellectual life thrown off by some gigantic act of generation performed upon that nest of knowledge, those inexhaustible ovaries of learning, the concentric inner rings of the catalogue shelves.

The circular wall of the Reading Room wrapped the scholars in a protective layer of books, while above them arched the vast, distended belly of the dome. Little daylight entered through the grimy glass at the top. No sounds of traffic or other human business penetrated to that warm, airless space. The dome looked down on the scholars, and the scholars looked down on their books; and the scholars loved their books, stroking the pages with soft pale fingers. The pages responded to the fingers' touch, and yielded their knowledge gladly to the scholars, who collected it in little boxes of file-cards. When the scholars raised their eyes from their desks they saw nothing to distract them, nothing out of harmony with their books, only the smooth, curved lining of the womb. Wherever the eye travelled, it met no arrest, no angle, no parallel lines receding into infinity, no pointed arch striving towards the unattainable: all was curved, rounded, self-sufficient, complete. And the scholars dropped their eyes to their books again, fortified and consoled. They curled themselves more tightly over their books, for they did not want to leave the warm womb, where they fed upon electric light and inhaled the musty odour of yellowing pages.

But the women who waited outside felt differently. From their dingy flats in Islington and cramped semis in Bexleyheath, they looked out through the windows at the life of the world, at the motor-cars and the advertisements and the clothes in the shops, and they found them good. And they resented the warm womb of the Museum which made them poor and lonely, which swallowed up their men every day and sapped them of their vital spirits and made them silent and abstracted mates even when they were at home. And the women sighed for the day when their men would be expelled from the womb for the last time, and they looked at their children whimpering at their feet, and they clasped their hands, coarsened with detergent, and vowed that these children would never be scholars.

Lawrence, thought Adam. It's time I got on to Lawrence.

He weaved his way to the row of desks where he and Camel usually worked, and noted the familiar figures at whose sides he had worked for two years, without ever exchanging word with any of them: earnest, efficient Americans, humming away like dynamos, powered by Guggenheim grants; turbaned Sikhs, all called Mr Singh, and all studying Indian influences on English literature; pimply, bespectacled women smiling cruelly to themselves as they noted an error in somebody's footnote; and then the Museum characters – the gentleman whose beard reached to his feet, the lady in shorts, the man wearing odd shoes and a yachting-cap reading a Gaelic newspaper with a one-stringed lute propped up on his desk, the woman who sniffed. Adam recognized Camel's coat and briefcase at one of the desks, but the seat was unoccupied.

Eventually he discovered Camel in the North Library. They did not usually work there: it was overheated, and its low rectangular shape and green furnishings gave one the sense of being in an aquarium for tropical fish. The North Library was used especially for consulting rare and valuable books, and there were also a number of seats reserved for the exclusive use of eminent scholars, who enjoyed the privilege of leaving their books on their desks for indefinite periods. These desks were rarely occupied except by piles of books and cards bearing distinguished names, and they reminded Adam of a waxworks from which all the exhibits had been withdrawn for renovation.

'What are you doing here?' he whispered to Camel.

'I'm reading an allegedly pornographic book,' Camel explained. 'You have to fill out a special application and read it here under the Superintendent's nose. To make sure you don't masturbate, I suppose.'

'Good Lord. D'you think they'll make me do that for *Lady Chatterley's Lover*?'

'Shouldn't think so, now you can buy it and masturbate at home.'

'What seat did you save for me in the Reading Room?'

'Next to mine. Number thirteen, I think.'

43

'You seem to have an attachment to the number thirteen where I'm concerned,' said Adam, petulantly. 'I'm not superstitious, but there's no point in taking chances.'

'What kind of chances?'

'Never mind,' said Adam.

He returned to the Reading Room and, wielding the huge volumes of the catalogue with practised ease, filled in application slips for *The Rainbow* and several critical studies of Lawrence. Then he returned to the seat Camel had saved for him, to wait. One of the Museum's many throwbacks to a more leisured and gracious age was that books were delivered to one's desk. So vast was the library, however – Adam understood it amounted to six million volumes – and so understaffed, that it was normal for more than an hour to elapse between the lodging of an application and the arrival of a book. He sat down on the large padded seat, ignoring the envious and accusing glances of the readers in his vicinity. For some reason only about one in ten of the Reading Room seats was padded, and there was fierce competition for the possession of them.

The padded seats were magnificently comfortable. Adam wondered whether they were made by Brownlong and Co. If so, he felt he could address himself to the competition with real enthusiasm.

> I always choose a Brownlong chair
> Because I wrote my thesis there.

The manufacturer's name was usually found on the underside of chairs, wasn't it? Adam wondered whether he might turn his chair upside down for inspection, but decided that it would attract too much attention. He looked round: no one was watching. He deliberately dropped a pencil on the floor, and bent down to recover it, peering under his seat the while. He dimly discerned a small nameplate but could not read the inscription. He put his head right under the seat, lost his balance and fell heavily to the floor. Startled, annoyed or amused faces were turned upon him from the neighbouring desks. Red with embarrassment and from the blood that had rushed to his head while he hung upside down, Adam recovered his seat and rubbed his head.

Adam was filled with self-pity. It was the second time that morning that he had fallen down. Then there were the hallucinations. Clearly, something was seriously the matter with him. He was approaching a nervous breakdown. He repeated the words to himself with a certain pleasure. Nervous. Breakdown. They evoked a prospect of peace and passivity, of helpless withdrawal from the world, of a huge burden of worry shifted on to someone else's shoulders. He saw himself lying mildly in a darkened room while anxious friends and doctors held whispered conferences round his bed. Perhaps they would make a petition to the Pope and get him and Barbara a special dispensation to practise artificial contraception. Or perhaps he would die, his tragic case be brought to the attention of the Vatican Council, and the doctrine of Natural Law revised as a result. A fat lot of good that would do *him*. Adam decided not to have a nervous breakdown after all.

To work, to work. He began briskly to unpack his bulging holdalls. Soon the broad, blue leather-topped desk was heaped with books, files, folders, index-cards and odd scraps of paper with notes and references scribbled on them. Adam's energy and determination subsided like the mercury of a thermometer plunged in cold water. How would he ever succeed in organizing all this into anything coherent?

The subject of Adam's thesis had originally been, 'Language and Ideology in Modern Fiction' but had been whittled down by the Board of Studies until it now stood as 'The Structure of Long Sentences in Three Modern English Novels'. The whittling down didn't seem to have made his task any easier. He still hadn't decided which three novels he was going to analyse, nor had he decided how long a long sentence was. Lawrence, he thought hopefully, would produce lots of sentences where the issue would not be in doubt.

Adam listlessly turned over pages of notes on minor novelists who were now excluded from his thesis. There was this great wad, for instance, on Egbert Merrymarsh, the Catholic belletrist, younger contemporary of Chesterton and Belloc. Adam had written a whole chapter, tentatively entitled 'The Divine Wisecrack' on Merrymarsh's use of paradox and antithesis to prop up his facile Christian apologetics. All wasted labour.

Adam yawned, and looked at the clock above the entrance to the North Library. There was still a long time to go before his books would arrive. Everyone but himself seemed to be working with quiet concentration: you could almost hear a faint hum of cerebral flywheels and sprockets busily turning. Adam was seized by conflicting emotions of guilt, envy, frustration and revolt. Revolt won: this still repose, this physical restraint, was unnatural.

He fiddled idly with his pencil, trying to make it stand on end. He failed, and the pencil fell to the floor. He stooped cautiously to recover it, meeting, as he straightened up, the frown of a distracted reader. Adam frowned back. Why shouldn't he be distracted? Distraction was as necessary to mental health as exercise to physical. It would be a good idea, in fact, if the Reading Room were cleared twice a day, and all the scholars marched out to do physical jerks in the forecourt. No, that wouldn't do – he hated physical jerks himself. Suppose, instead, the circular floor of the Reading Room were like the revolve on a stage, and that every hour, on the hour, the Superintendent would throw a lever to set the whole thing in motion, sweeping the spokes of the desks round for a few exhilarating revolutions. Yes, and the desks would be mounted so as to go gently up and down like horses on a carousel. It wouldn't necessarily interrupt work – just give relief to the body cramped in the same position. Tone up the system. Encourage the circulation. Yes, he must remember to mention it to Camel. The British Museum Act. He closed his eyes and indulged in a pleasing vision of the gay scene, as the floor rotated, and the scholars smiled with quiet pleasure at each other as their seats rose above the partitions, and gently sank again. Perhaps there might be tinkling music . . .

Adam felt a tap on his shoulder. It was Camel.

'Why are you humming "La Ronde"? You're getting some black looks.'

'I'll tell you later,' said Adam, in some confusion. He fled from the Reading Room to avoid the hostile glances directed at him from all sides.

In the foyer, he decided to ring Barbara again. To his surprise, the booth was still occupied by the fat man. Adam was beginning to make awed calculations of the cost of a thirty-minute call to Colorado, when his attention was caught by various signs of distress the fat man was making. He had somehow managed to close the door of the booth, which folded inwards, but his girth rendered him incapable of opening it again. After some moments of strenuous exertion, Adam was able to extricate him.

'Well,' said the fat man. 'You seem to be my private boy scout today.'

'Did you make your phone call all right?' Adam inquired.

'I experienced some linguistic difficulties.'

'Don't they speak English in Colorado?'

'Sure they do. But your operator kept saying, "You're through" before I'd even started . . . do you smoke cigars?' he suddenly demanded.

'My father-in-law usually gives me one on Christmas Day,' said Adam.

'Well, save these and astonish him in December,' said the fat man, thrusting a fistful of huge cigars into Adam's breast pocket.

'Thank you,' murmured Adam faintly, as the fat man trundled off.

'Thank *you*!'

Adam entered the phone booth, which smelled suspiciously of rich cigar smoke, and made his call. There was a clatter as the receiver was lifted at the other end, and a childish voice intoned:

'Battersea Double Two One – O.'

'Oh hallo, Clare darling. What are you doing at the phone?'

'Mummy said I could practise answering.'

'Is Mummy there?'

'She's just coming down the stairs.'

'And how are you, Clare? Have you been a good girl this morning?'

'No.'

'Oh. Why's that?'

'I cut a hole in Dominic's tummy.'

'You *what?*'

'Cut a hole in Dominic's tummy. With the kitchen scissors.'

'But Clare, *why?*' Adam wailed.

'We were playing maternity hospitals and I was giving him a Caesarian.'

'But Clare, you mustn't do that.'

'You mean boys can't have babies? I know.'

'No, I mean cut people with scissors. Look, is Mummy there?'

'Here she is.'

'Hallo, Adam?'

'Darling, what's all this about Clare cutting a hole in Dominic's stomach?'

'It's only a nick. It didn't even bleed.'

'Only a nick! But what was she doing with the scissors in the first place?'

'Are you trying to blame me, Adam?'

'No, darling. I'm just trying to get at the facts.'

'As long as you're not trying to blame me. You've no idea what it's like having to look after Clare all day.'

'I know, I know. But if you could just keep the scissors out of her reach . . .'

'I do. She got the step-ladder out.'

'Did you smack her?'

'You know smacking doesn't have any effect on Clare. She just says, "I hope this is doing *you* good, Mummy." She's heard us discussing Doctor Spock.'

'God help us when she learns to read,' sighed Adam. He decided to drop the subject. 'Have you looked up the 13th in your diary?'

'You'll wish you hadn't asked.'

'Why?' said Adam, his heart sinking.

'According to the chart, ovulation should have taken place about then.'

Adam groaned.

'. . . And the 13th was a Friday,' continued Barbara.

'This is no time for joking,' said Adam, suspiciously.

'Who's joking?'

'I'm certainly not. Can't you remember anything about that night?'

'I remember you were a bit . . . you know.'

'A bit what?'

'You know what you're like when you've had a few drinks.'

'You're just the same,' said Adam defensively.

'I'm not blaming you.'

'D'you think we could have . . .?'

'No. But I wish my period would start.'

'How do you feel now?'

'About the same.'

'What was that? I've forgotten.'

'Never mind. I'm getting bored with the subject. Shouldn't you be working.'

'I can't work while I'm trying to think what we did that night.'

'Well, I can't help you, Adam. Look, I can't stay any longer. Mary Flynn is bringing her brood round for lunch.'

'How many has she got now?'

'Four.'

'Well, there's always someone else worse off than yourself.'

'Good-bye then, darling. And try not to worry.'

'Good-bye, darling.'

On his way back to the Reading Room, Adam had a thought. He returned to the phone booth and rang Barbara again.

'Hallo, darling.'

'Adam, for heaven's sake –'

'Look, I've had a thought. About that night. Did you happen to notice the sheets the next day . . .?'

Barbara rang off. This is denaturing me, he thought.

He was getting tired with trekking backwards and forwards to the telephone. After the coolness of the foyer, the atmosphere of the Reading Room, when he re-entered it, struck him as oppressively hot. The dome seemed screwed down tightly on the stale air, sealing it in. It hung over the scene like a tropical sky before a storm; and the faint, sour smell of mouldering books and bindings was like the reek of rotting vegetation in some foetid oriental backwater. Appleby cast a gloomy eye on the Indians and Africans working busily in their striped suits and starched collars.

There comes a moment in the life of even the most un-imaginative man – and Appleby was not that – when Destiny confronts him with the unexpected and the inexplicable, when the basis of his universe, like a chair which has so habitually offered its comforting support to his limbs that he no longer troubles to assure himself of its presence before entrusting his weight to it, is silently and swiftly withdrawn, and the victim feels himself falling with dismaying velocity into an infinite space of doubt. This was the sensation of Appleby as, mopping away with a soiled handkerchief the perspiration which beaded his forehead like the drops of moisture on the interior of a ship's hull that warn the knowledgeable mariner that he is approaching the equatorial line, he came in sight of the desk where he had left his books and papers. He staggered to a halt.

That *was* his desk, surely? Yes, he recognized on the one next to it his comrade's raincoat and broad-brimmed trilby. His own belongings, however, had vanished: his books, papers, index-cards – all had disappeared. But it was not this fact which made Appleby lean against a bookcase for support, and pass his right hand several times across his eyes. Grouped round his desk, and gazing at it with rapt attention, were three Chinese: not the Westernized, Hong Kong Chinese he was familiar with, draped in American-style suits and wielding sophisticated cameras, but authentic Chinese Chinese, dressed in loose, belted uniforms of some drab, coarse-grained material.

It was their attitude, above all, which made the hair on Appleby's nape prickle as at the brush of a passing ghost – an attitude which suggested prayer rather than conspiracy, and was the more frightening because the more unaccountable. If they were waiting for him, why were their backs turned, why were they poring, with bowed heads and hands clasped behind their backs, upon the bare expanse of his desk? It was as if they were engaged in some hypocritical act of mourning for a crime they had already committed.

Appleby perceived that the strangers' presence had not gone unnoticed by the other readers in the vicinity, but it seemed almost as if the latter were trying to pretend otherwise. Without lifting their heads from their books, they were stealing glances, first at the Chinese, and then at himself. An African law student, sitting near him, rolled a white eye and seemed about to speak, but thought the better of it and turned back to his books. If only, Adam felt, he could see the faces of his visitors, he would know what they had come for. He shrank from the encounter, but anything was preferable to the mystery. Or was it . . .? If he were to walk away, go home and think about it, and come back later, tomorrow say, perhaps they would have gone away, and his books would be back on the desk, and he could forget all about it. As he stood wavering at this fork in the road of his moral self-exploration, he was suddenly relieved of the choice by a light tap on his shoulder and a voice which murmured, 'Mr Appleby?'

4

I believe there are several persons in a state of imbecility
who come to read in the British Museum. I have been informed
that there are several in that state who are sent there by their
friends to pass away their time.

Carlyle

'So it appeared,' said Adam, biting into a Scotch egg, 'that these
Chinese were some cultural delegation or something from Com-
munist China, and that they'd asked if they could look at Karl
Marx's desk – you know, the one he worked at when he was
researching *Das Kapital*. Did you know that, Camel? That you
saved me Karl Marx's seat?'

Camel, whose face was buried in a pint tankard, tried to shake
his head and spilled a few drops of beer on his trousers.

'I should have thought it would have singed your good
Catholic arse,' said Pond.

'It makes you think, doesn't it?' Adam mused. 'All the
famous backsides who have polished those seats: Marx, Ruskin,
Carlyle . . .'

'Colin Wilson,' suggested Pond.

'Who?' Adam asked.

'Before your time, old boy,' said Camel. 'The good old days
of the Museum, when everyone was writing books on the
Human Condition and publishers were fighting under the desks
for the options.'

'You'd think you only had to sit at any of those desks,' Adam went on, 'and the wisdom would just seep up through your spinal cord. It just seems to seep out of mine. Look at today, for instance; lunch time and I haven't done a thing.'

They were in the Museum Tavern, Adam, Camel and Pond. Pond was a full-time teacher at the School of English where Camel taught a few evening classes. It was run by a crook, and Pond was worked very hard, but Adam and Camel found it difficult to commiserate with him because he earned so very much money. He and his pretty wife, Sally, had a Mini-Minor and a centrally-heated semi in Norwood with a four-poster bed draped in pink satin. Pond usually lunched with Adam and Camel one day a week, among other things in order to rid himself of the xenophobia which, as he explained, was both an occupational state of mind and a professional crime. According to Camel, he was the soul of kindness to his foreign pupils while on the job.

'That's because Karl Marx was a Jew,' he now said in reply to Adam's complaint. 'All you have to do is change your seat.'

'That's right,' said Camel, 'find yourself the seat Chesterton used. Or Belloc.'

'Or Egbert Merrymarsh,' said Adam.

'Who?'

'Who?'

'Before your time,' said Adam. 'The good old days of the Museum, when there was a crucifix on every desk. The trouble is,' he went on, 'that Merrymarsh probably chose an unpadded seat, just to mortify himself.'

'So what about the Chinese?' said Camel. 'What did you say to them?'

'Well, I was just summing up courage to go up to them and say . . . say . . . well, say something, I don't know, like, this is my seat, or, what have you done with my books, when this superintendent came up and explained. He'd been looking for me, but I was telephoning Barbara.'

'He's always telephoning his wife,' explained Camel to Pond.

'Well, that's all right; I like to phone Sally myself occasionally,' said Pond.

'Ah, that's just uxoriousness. Appleby is a neurotic case.'

'I'm not neurotic,' said Adam. 'I toyed with the idea this morning, but I decided against it. Though, I must admit, those Chinese had me worried for a minute.'

'Chinks,' said Pond. 'Don't be afraid of good old prejudiced English usage.'

'I must say, whoever it was had a nerve removing your books,' said Camel.

'Oh, I could see their point. Like tidying up a grave or something.'

Pond shuddered, as he always did at the mention of death, and swigged some beer.

'What exactly did the Superintendent say to you?' Camel asked. 'I want to know exactly what he said. Did he say, "I hope you won't mind, but three Chinese gentlemen are looking at your desk"?'

'Yes, he did, actually,' said Adam, surprised. 'That's exactly what he did say.'

'And what did you say?'

'I didn't say anything at first. I tell you, I felt pretty queer.'

'So what happened then?'

'Well, he looked a bit embarrassed, and said, "It was Karl Marx's desk, you see. We often get visitors wanting to see it." '

'So what did you say then?'

'Well, that's what I was going to tell you. I *think* I said: *Mr Marx, he dead!*'

Camel and Pond looked meaningfully at each other. 'I told you,' said Camel. 'Appleby is cracking up.'

'I can see,' said Pond, 'he's going to become one of the Museum eccentrics. Before we know it, he'll be shuffling around in slippers and muttering into a beard.'

'It's a special form of scholarly neurosis,' said Camel. 'He's no longer able to distinguish between life and literature.'

'Oh yes I can,' said Adam. 'Literature is mostly about having sex and not much about having children. Life is the other way round.'

Pond came back from the bar carrying three pints.

'That's funny,' said Adam. 'You're limping.'

'What's funny about that?'

'Well, I'm limping too.'

'Perhaps it's a bug that's going round,' said Camel.

'I don't think, somehow,' said Pond, 'that our symptoms have the same cause.'

'I don't even know the cause of mine,' said Adam. 'I just woke up this morning with a pain in my leg.'

'Why are *you* limping, then?' Camel asked Pond.

Pond made a grimace. 'That damned *Kama Sutra*,' he said, in the tone of a man boasting of his hereditary gout. 'I forget which position it was – the Monkey or the Goose or something. I know I got a terrible cramp. Took Sally an hour's rubbing with Sloane's Liniment to straighten me out.'

'I hope it will teach you a lesson,' said Camel.

'It was worth it,' replied Pond, winking.

'My God!' Adam exclaimed. 'You mean you're so sated with conventional sex . . . Pardon me while my imagination boggles.'

'It's that four-poster bed that does it,' Camel opined. 'The pink drapes.'

'No, as a matter of fact I think it's the central heating,' said Pond. 'You've no idea how central heating extends the possibilities of sex.'

'Be a waste of money for us, then,' said Adam gloomily.

'Well, drink up,' urged Pond. 'Bloody wogs.'

'Bloody wogs,' they murmured. Pond insisted on this toast

56

when he drank with them. It was only a matter of time, Adam thought, before someone heard them and insisted on their expulsion from the Tavern.

'You know,' said Camel to Adam, 'I think you ought to apostatize. You can't go on like this.'

'What d'you mean?'

'Well, leave the Church – temporarily I mean. You can go back to it later.'

'Death-bed repentance, you mean?'

'Well, more of a menopause repentance. It's not such a risk is it? You and Barbara have a good expectation of living past forty or so.'

'It's no good talking to him like that, Camel,' said Pond. 'There's always the bus.'

'Yes, there's always the bus,' Adam agreed.

'Bus? What bus?' asked Camel in bewilderment.

'The bus that runs you down. The death that comes un-expectedly,' explained Pond. 'Catholics are brought up to expect sudden extinction round every corner and to keep their souls highly polished at all times.'

'How do you know all this?' Adam demanded.

'Sally went to a convent,' Pond explained. 'No,' he went on, 'it's no use talking like that to Adam. We've got to convince him intellectually that Catholicism is false.'

'I wouldn't want to do that,' said Camel. 'I believe in religion. I don't have any myself, but I believe in other people having religion.'

'And children,' Adam interpolated.

'Quite so,' Camel agreed. 'I don't have any affection for chil-dren myself, but I recognize the need for them to keep the human show on the road.'

'Selfish bastard,' said Adam.

'But if you must have religion,' said Pond, 'why not Hinduism? Then you can have sex as well.'

'I thought you were against things foreign,' said Camel.

'Well, I think we could have a kind of Anglicized Hinduism . . . get rid of the holy cows and so on.'

'No, it won't do,' said Camel. 'I want Christianity kept up, because otherwise half our literary heritage will disappear. We need people like Appleby to tell us what *The Cloud of Unknowing* is all about.'

'Never heard of it,' said Adam.

'Or the *Ancrene Rewle*.'

'That's what let me down in my Middle English paper,' said Adam.

'You should read it sometime. There's some very interesting cloacal imagery in it.'

'But Camel,' said Pond, 'for your purposes, it's quite enough if people have a Christian education. There's no need for them to practise the darn thing all their lives. We owe it to Adam to free him from the shackles of a superstitious creed.'

'Go ahead, convince me,' Adam invited.

Pond, who fancied himself as a logician, shifted his chair nearer the table, and leaned his elbows upon it, pressing the fingers of each hand lightly together.

'Very good,' applauded Camel. 'The fingers is very good. First round to Pond.'

Pond ignored the diversion. 'Let's begin with the Trinity,' he said. 'The fundamental doctrine, as I understand it, of orthodox Christianity.'

'Doesn't give me much trouble,' said Adam, 'but go ahead.'

'It doesn't give you much trouble, if you don't mind my saying so, my dear Adam, because you don't think about it. In fact you don't really believe it, because your assent is never tested. Since it costs you nothing to accept the idea of three in one, you have never bothered to inquire why you *should* accept anything so utterly contrary to logic and experience. Now just remind yourself, for a moment, of the concept of number. See: one' – he placed a salt cellar in the centre of the table – 'two' – he placed a pepper pot beside it – 'three' – he reached for the mustard.

'I should have brought my clover leaf with me,' said Adam. He spooned some mustard on to his plate, and sprinkled it with pepper and salt. 'Three in one.'

'There!' cried Camel. 'It really tastes horrible, but it's true.'

'I think you're being highly irresponsible, Camel,' said Pond testily. 'Encouraging him like this. Especially as you propose remaining sterile yourself. Do you realize that the birth-rate figures show that England will be a predominantly Catholic country in three or four generations? Do you want that?'

'No,' said Adam fervently. 'But it won't happen because of the lapsation rate.'

'Lapsation?' Camel inquired.

'Falling off from the Church,' Adam explained.

'Why do so many fall off?'

'Not because of the doctrine of the Trinity,' said Adam. 'Because of birth control is my guess. Which reminds me: I have to attend a Dollinger meeting on that very subject this lunch hour. I must hurry.'

The Dollinger Society took its name from the celebrated German theologian of the nineteenth century who had been excommunicated in 1871 for his refusal to accept the doctrine of Papal Infallibility. Originally founded to press for the posthumous reversal of Dollinger's excommunication, and eventually his canonization (in pursuance of which unlikely objectives the founder-members had encouraged themselves by citing the precedent of Joan of Arc) it had since become an informal discussion group of lay Catholics concerned to liberalize the Church's attitude on more urgent and topical issues, such as religious liberty in Spain, nuclear war, and the Index Librorum Prohibitorum. Its only public activity took the form of writing outspoken letters on such subjects to the Catholic Press. The letters were never published, except in *Crypt*, a subscription newsletter edited by the Society's unofficial chaplain, Father Bill Wildfire OP, who, after a few beers, could be coaxed into questioning the doctrine of the Virgin Mary's Assumption into heaven. Heretical statements like this, particularly when they had a sacerdotal – or, better still, episcopal – origin, were a source of unholy joy to the Society, circulating among the members much like dirty jokes in secular fraternities. It often seemed to Adam that many Dollingerites declined to follow the example of their patron mainly because the liberal conscience had a more thrilling existence within the Church than outside it.

Adam attended the Society's meetings only spasmodically, but today's had a special interest for him. He wished that he had a clearer head for it. He had consumed more beer than he had been aware of. He staggered slightly, crossing the road between the Tavern and the Museum, and this decided him to walk rather than use his scooter. In any case, the distance was so short that it was scarcely worth the trouble of starting the scooter.

With characteristic daring, the Dollinger Society held its meetings in Student Christian Hall, an inter-denominational centre located in one of the tall, narrow houses in Gordon Square. It had a small canteen in the basement where homely young women served cottage pie and a peculiarly vivid form of tomato soup to anyone who offered himself as a student or a Christian. On the first floor was a reading room, and on the second a lounge, where the Dollingerites gathered once a month for coffee and discussion.

The meeting was already in progress when Adam arrived. He tiptoed across the floor and sank into a vacant armchair. About a dozen people were present. Adam could tell which of them had lunched downstairs by their orange moustaches. The secretary of the Society, Francis Maple, who was sub-manager of a Catholic bookshop, was evidently reading out the draft of a letter to the Catholic Press.

... advances in psychological knowledge and the increasing personalization of human relations in different aspects of life have also contributed to a new awareness of the positive contribution made by affective and physical elements in the attainment of marital harmony. Ordered human sexuality, within the legitimate framework of married life, undoubtedly contributes to the development of the whole person ...

It was a long letter. As it went on, Adam grew more and more impatient. It was not that these were bad arguments. They were good arguments. He had often used them himself. But their style of high-minded generality, their elevated concern with the fulfilment of the married vocation, somehow missed the real nub of the problem as it was felt by the individual: the ache of unsatisfied desire, or the pall of anxiety that the Safe Method draped over the marriage bed ... Perhaps the new refinements of temperature charts and whatever really did work, but no one who had experienced an unwanted pregnancy could really trust periodic abstinence. *Post coitum, omne animal triste est*, agreed; but not *before* coition, or for *days* afterwards.

The letter came to an end. After a long silence a flat-chested girl with ginger hair said, as she said on every similar occasion: 'Can't we bring the Mystical Body in somewhere?'

'Why?' Adam demanded. He was surprised by his own belligerence: it must be the beers. The ginger-haired girl cringed; her flat chest became concave. Adam felt sorry for her, but heard himself going on, 'It seems to me that we're concerned with the carnal body here.'

'I agree,' said a young man who had recently left a monastery and got engaged before his tonsure had grown over. 'We'll never get anything done until we have compulsory marriage of the clergy. They just don't understand.'

'Robert and I,' said his fiancée, 'think we should adopt Catholic orphans, instead of having children of our own. But with the present teaching on birth control it would be too risky. We might be overrun.'

There were sympathetic murmurs from the rest of the company. The fiancée looked pleased at the effect she had created.

'I'd like to know,' said Adam, 'what it is we want. I mean, do we want to use contraceptives, or the pill, or what? The letter didn't say.'

There was a slightly embarrassed silence. Francis Maple cleared his throat, and said:

'I think the letter was just intended to air the concern of Catholic lay people, and draw the clergy's attention to the subject.'

'Does anyone know,' said a bald-headed lawyer, the father of five, 'whether the pill is really allowed or not? I've heard there's a priest in Camden Town who recommends it in the confessional.'

'What's his name?' said half a dozen voices simultaneously.

'I don't know,' confessed the lawyer.

'As I understand it,' said Francis Maple, 'you can use a pill to regulate the female cycle and make the Safe Period Safer, but you're not allowed to use it to induce sterility.'

'I've heard the pill can make a woman grow a beard,' said a postgraduate student from Bedford College. 'Or make her pregnant when she's seventy,' she added, with a shudder.

'I'd like to know,' said the ex-monk, 'what Mr Appleby wants.'

Adam shifted uneasily in his seat, as the eyes of all present turned curiously on him.

'I don't know,' he said at length. 'I don't suppose anyone really *wants* to use contraceptives, even non-Catholics. They're not things you can work up much affection for, are they? Everybody seems to act a bit furtive about the business. Perhaps the pill will be the solution, but we don't know enough about it yet. What we want is emergency measures to deal with the present situation, while the theologians and the scientists thrash out the question of the pill. At the moment the situation is that we Catholics expend most of our moral energy on keeping or breaking the Church's teaching on birth control, when there are a lot of much more important moral issues in life.'

'Hear, hear!' said a lady whose pet cause was protesting against the Irish export of horses for slaughter.

'The trouble with using contraceptives, from the point of view of practical moral theology,' Adam went on, wondering what conclusion he was going to reach, 'is that it's necessarily a premeditated sin. You can biff someone on the head or seduce someone's wife at a party, and go to confession and say, "Father, I was overcome by my passions," and be sincerely sorry, and promise not to do it again, and do the same thing a week later without being a hypocrite. But the other thing is something you commit, in the first place, in cold blood in a chemist's shop; and once you start you have to go on steadily, or there's no point.'

'That's very well put,' said Maple, as Adam recovered his breath. 'But what can we do about it?'

'The only thing I can see is to get contraception classified as a venial sin,' said Adam, with sudden inspiration. 'Then we could all feel slightly guilty about it, like cheating on the buses, without forfeiting the sacraments.'

This proposition seemed to take the group by surprise, and a long silence ensued.

'Well,' said Francis Maple at length, 'that's a novel point of view certainly. I don't know if there's any machinery for classifying sins . . . But there's a general consensus which can be modified, I suppose.'

At this point the door burst open, and Father Wildfire entered.

'Ah!' said Maple, with relief. 'You come at an opportune moment, Father.'

'Why, somebody dying?' said the priest, with a boisterous laugh.

'No, it's just that we're getting into rather deep theological waters. Adam, here, thinks that the birth control problem could be solved if contraception were just considered as a venial sin.'

'Isn't it?' said Father Wildfire, with feigned surprise. The group laughed delightedly, but discreetly, as if they were in church. 'Is there anything to drink?' asked the priest, unbuttoning his coat. This was a rough serge jacket of the kind worn by building labourers. Underneath it he wore a red woollen shirt and brown corduroy trousers. The Dominicans appeared to have very liberal regulations, of which Father Wildfire took full advantage, concerning the wearing of the habit. Adam often thought that if, as seemed likely, he was eventually de-frocked, no one would ever know it.

A cup of coffee was passed to the priest, who extracted a small flask from his pocket, and poured a generous measure into the cup. 'Seriously,' he said, 'this venial sin–mortal sin business is old hat. Something the scholastics thought up to while away the long winter evenings. All sins are mortal sins. Or, to put it another way, all sins are venial sins. What matters is love. The more love, the less sin. I was preaching at a men's retreat the other day, and I told them, better sleep with a prostitute with some kind of love than with your wife out of habit. Seems some of them took me at my word, and the bishop is rather cross.'

Adam wanted to ask if it was better to make love to your wife using a contraceptive, or not to make love to her at all; but somehow it did not seem an appropriate question to ask Father Wildfire. He lived at the frontiers of the spiritual life, where dwelt criminals, prostitutes, murderers and saints, a territory steaming with the fumes of human iniquity, from which souls emerged, if they emerged at all, toughened and purified by a heroic struggle with evil. In contrast, Adam's moral problem seemed trivial and suburban, and to seek Father Wildfire's advice would be like engaging the services of a big-game hunter to catch a mouse.

The circle of Dollingerites had now broken up into small

groups, the most numerous of which was clustered round Father Wildfire, who was expatiating on the problems of Irish girls who came to London to have their illegitimate babies. Thinking of his own healthy and tolerably happy family, Adam was stricken with self-reproach. A favourite remark of his mother's, 'There's always someone worse off than yourself,' stirred in his memory. He found the maxim no more efficacious in removing anxiety now than it had been in the past. Healthy and happy his family might be, but only so long as it stood at a manageable number. Already the problem of supporting them was formidable. He really must begin to think seriously about jobs for next year.

It was cold and damp on the pavement outside Student Christian Hall. The leafless trees in Gordon Square stood black and gaunt against the façade of Georgian houses. The sky was cold and grey. It looked like snow.

I hunched my shoulders inside my coat and set off briskly in the direction of the English Department (Adam Appleby might have written). I had an appointment with Briggs, my supervisor. He was a punctual man, and appreciated punctuality in others. I mean that he liked people to be on time. Men who have sacrificed a lot of big things to their careers often cling fiercely to small habits.

Access to the English Department was through a small court-yard at the rear of the College. There seemed to be a lot of young people about, and I had to linger some moments before I caught the eye of Jones, the Beadle. I always make a point of catching the eye of beadles, porters and similar servants. Jones did not disappoint me: his face lit up.

'Hallo, sir. Haven't seen you for some time.'

'Come to see Mr Briggs, Jones. There seem to be a lot of people about?'

'Undergraduates, sir,' he explained.

The English Department wasn't the most distinguished build-ing in the College, but it had history. The brick façade, stained with soot and streaked with rain water, was thought to be a good example of its type, which was turn-of-the-century warehousing. When, some thirty years ago, the expanding College had bought the freehold, rather than demolish the building they had skilfully converted the interior into classrooms and narrow, cell-like offices by means of matchboard partitions. It wasn't what you could call a comfortable or elegant building, but it had character. Its small, grimy windows looked on to an identical building twenty feet away, which housed the Department of Civil Engineering. But, schooled by long practice, I turned into the right door and mounted the long stone staircase.

The door of Briggs's room on the second floor was open, and the sound of conversation floated into the corridor. I tapped on the door and extended my head into the room.

'Oh, come in, Appleby,' said Briggs.

He was talking to Bane, who had recently been appointed to a new Chair of Absurdist Drama, endowed by a commercial television company. This, I knew, had been a blow to Briggs, who was the senior man of the two, and who had been looking about for a Chair for some time. His own field was the English Essay. No one was likely to endow a special Chair in the English Essay, and Briggs knew it. His best chance of promotion lay in the retirement of the Head of Department, old Howells, who was always raising Briggs's expectations by retreating at the beginning of term to a Swiss sanatorium, only to dash them again by returning refreshed and reinvigorated at the beginning of the vacations.

The posture of the two men seemed to illustrate their relationship. Bane was sprawled in Briggs's lumpy armchair, his legs stretched out over the brown linoleum. Briggs stood by the window, uneasily fingering the ridges of the radiator. On his desk was an open bottle of British sherry. At my appearance he seemed to straighten up his tired, slack body, and to become his usual efficient, slightly fussy self.

'Come in, come in,' he repeated.

'I don't want to interrupt you . . .'

'No, come in. You know Professor Bane, of course?'

Bane nodded casually, but affably enough. 'How's the research going?' he asked.

'I hope to start writing soon,' I replied.

'Will you take a glass of sherry wine?' said Briggs, who affected such redundancies in his speech.

'Thank you, but I've already lunched,' I explained.

Briggs glanced at his watch. 'I suppose it *is* late. What does your wrist-watch say, Bane?'

'A quarter to two.'

'We've been talking, and forgot the time,' said Briggs. If Briggs was losing his habit of punctuality, I thought, he must be seriously affected by the promotion of Bane.

Bane got up and stretched himself nonchalantly. 'Well, I think we've talked it out now,' he said. 'Perhaps you'll think it over, Briggs, and let me know what you decide.'

Briggs bit his lip, at the same time pulling nervously on the lobes of both ears. It was a little nervous habit of his which you didn't notice at first.

'I must say,' he said, 'it surprises me a little that the Prof hasn't mentioned this to me at all.'

Bane shrugged. 'Of course, you realize that it means nothing to me, and the last thing I want to do is to put you to any inconvenience. But it seems that the Prof wants all the people with Chairs' – he leaned slightly on the word – 'together on one floor. I think you'll find my little room on the fourth floor quite snug. At least one doesn't suffer from interruptions up there. Put it this way: you'll be able to get on with your book,' he concluded maliciously. Briggs had been working for twenty years on a history of the English Essay.

As Briggs opened his mouth to reply, he was forestalled by a frenzied crashing in the radiator pipes, emanating from the boilers far below, but filling the room with such a din as to render speech inaudible. While the racket continued, the three of us stood, motionless and silent, lost in our own thoughts. I felt a certain thrill at being witness to one of those classic struggles for power and prestige which characterize the lives of ambitious men and which, in truth, exhaust most of their time and energy. To the casual observer, it might seem that nothing important was at stake here, but it might well be that the future course of English studies in the University hung upon this conversation.

At length the noise in the radiator pipes diminished, and faded away. Briggs said:

'I'm glad you mentioned my book, Bane. To be honest with you, the thing I have most against a move is my collection here.' Briggs gestured towards the huge, ugly, worm-eaten bookcase that housed his collection of the English essayists: Addison, Steele, Johnson, Lamb, Hazlitt, Belloc, Chesterton . . . even Egbert Merrymarsh was represented here by a slim, white-buckram volume privately printed by Carthusian monks on hand-made paper. 'I just don't see how it will fit into your room,' explained Briggs.

This was Briggs's trump-card. His collection was famous, and no one would dare to suggest that he break it up. Bane lost his nonchalant air, and looked cross: a faint flush coloured his pouchy cheeks. 'I'll get Jones to take some measurements,' he said abruptly, and left the room.

Briggs brightened momentarily at Bane's departure, no doubt consoled by the thought that Jones was in his own pocket. But the hidden pressures of the discussion had taken their toll, and he seemed a tired and defeated man as he sank into his desk-chair.

'Well,' he said at length, 'how's the research going?'

'I hope to start writing soon,' I replied. 'But I fear I won't be able to submit in June. I think I'll have to get an extension to October.'

'That's a pity, Appleby, a great pity. I disapprove of theses running on and on. Look at Camel, for instance.'

'Yes, I know. What worries me is the question of jobs. I really will need a job next academic year.'

'A job? A university post, is it that you want, Appleby?'

'Yes, I –'

I was about to allude delicately to the possibility of a vacancy in the Department, caused by Bane's new Chair, when Briggs went on, with startling emphasis:

'Then I have only one word of advice to you, Appleby. Publish! Publish or perish! That's how it is in the academic world these days. There was a time when appointments were made on a more human basis, but not any more.'

'The snag is, nothing I have is quite ready for publication . . .'

With an effort, Briggs dragged his attention away from his private discontents and brought it to bear on mine. But the energy went out of his voice, and he seemed bored.

'What about that piece you showed me on Merrymarsh?' he said vaguely.

'Do you really think . . . It's my impression there's not much interest in Merrymarsh these days.'

'Interest? Interest doesn't matter, as long as you get it published. Who do you suppose is interested in Absurdist drama?'

I left Briggs staring moodily into his empty sherry-glass. On my way out of the building I met Bane again, and took the opportunity to ask his advice on a trivial bibliographical problem. He seemed flattered by the inquiry, and took me up to his room to look up the reference.

When I finally made my departure, the trees were still there in Gordon Square, bleak and gaunt against the Georgian façade. I walked back to the Museum under a cold grey sky. I wondered idly which man I disliked most, Briggs or Bane.

5

I spent my days at the British Museum, and must, I think, have
been very delicate, for I remember often putting off hour after hour
consulting some necessary book because I shrank from lifting the
heavy volumes of the catalogue.

W. B. Yeats

As Adam approached the British Museum, lethargy and despair
oppressed him. By now, a pile of Lawrence books would be on
his desk, but he felt no quickening of his pulse at the prospect. In
Great Russell Street he lingered outside the windows of bookshops, stationers and small publishers. The stationers particularly
fascinated him. He coveted the files, punches, staplers, erasers,
coloured inks and gadgets whose functions remained a teasing
mystery, thinking that if only he could afford to equip himself
with all this apparatus his thesis would write itself: he would be
automated.

Feeling a faint pang of hunger – the Scotch egg in the Tavern
seemed very distant – Adam entered a small shop near the corner
of Museum Street, and purchased a bar of chocolate. A headline
in the evening paper about the Vatican Council caught his eye,
and he bought a copy. He crossed the road and passed through
the gates of the Museum, which sat massively before him, its
wings like arms extended to sweep him into the yawning, gap-
toothed maw of the portico. As he mounted the steps, Adam
decided not to be swallowed immediately. He sat down on one
of the benches in the colonnade and munched his chocolate,

glancing at the newspaper. Cardinal Suenens, he was glad to see, had called for a radical re-examination of the Church's teaching on birth control. Cardinal Ottavianik had countered by asserting that married Catholics should place their trust in Divine Providence. On no other issue, the paper's correspondent reported, were the liberal and conservative factions at the Council so clearly defined. A prolonged and bitter debate was in prospect, which was likely to be resolved only by the personal intervention of the Pope, who had not as yet indicated the direction of his own thinking on the matter.

A chill breeze blew round Adam's neck. He raised the hood of his duffle coat and muffled his hands in the sleeves. The hood came down over his head like a monk's cowl. He gazed between the massive Ionic pillars at the vacant courtyard, and saw it thronged with cheering crowds under a blue Italian sky . . .

* * * Indeed it was a day of days, *Father Francesco Francescini, humble member of the Papal household, wrote in his diary,* and I bless the Divine Providence which ordained that I, a humble Franciscan friar, should have been privy to its tremendous doings. Not merely the election of a new Pope – but an English Pope, the first for eight centuries – and not merely an English Pope, but an English Pope who has been married! Little did the Fathers of the Council suspect, I wager, when they approved by so narrow a margin the admission of married men to Holy Orders, that they would soon be acclaiming a Supreme Pontiff with four *bambini*. Most mirific! Astonishing are the ways of God.

I would give my rosary beads, carved from the shin-bone of holy St Francis himself, to know what struggles in the Conclave brought about the election of this unknown Padre Appleby, secretary to the English Cardinal and, they say, ordained but lately, to the highest office of Holy Church. Whatever the true history (and the Conclave's vow of secrecy ensures that it will never be known, not for some days anyway) it is accomplished.

We have a Pope! *Habemus Papam!* With what a sour face old Scarlettofeverini, despot of the Holy Office, enunciated the longed-for words to the cheering multitude in St Peter's Square, who for days had watched the black smoke of disagreement floating into the sky above the Sistine chapel. Just before the announcement, in the Papal chamber behind the balcony, he had inquired, with a vulpine snarl, what name the new Pope proposed to take.

'We take the name of Alexander,' said the Pope with deliberation. The Sacred College reeled back in dismay. There was a flutter of ringed hands, a squeaking and cawing as of startled birds.

'*Alexander!*' hissed Scarlettofeverini. 'Will you make a mockery of the Papacy that you take the name of the most infamous man who ever disgraced its annals?'

'Alexander the Sixth was the last Pope to be the father of children,' replied the Pope, with marble poise. 'Let us hope that in these more enlightened times Alexander the Seventh may show such a circumstance is not incompatible with the proper government of the Church.'

Alexander the Seventh! Long may he reign!

This evening Sister Maria of the Sacred Heart, housekeeper to the late Pope, came to me in perturbation. It seems the new Pontiff had requested some Scottish delicacy, compounded of egg and sausage, unknown to the kitchen staff. I recommended that the Scottish College be consulted.* * *

* * * After only a few days our new Pope has already won the hearts of the Roman people. At first there was a natural suspicion of this unknown Englishman, but the astonishing sight of the Holy Father riding his diminutive scooter through the streets of Rome, skilfully controlling the machine with his left hand while he scatters blessings with his right, his white robes floating in the breeze like the wings of the Holy Ghost, has endeared him to all and sundry. In particular, it is noted with approval that he

favours a scooter of Italian design, albeit an antiquated and unreliable model which, with characteristic humility, he declines to exchange for a new one.

Memo: to confess that I broke my fast today to sample the Scottish egg. Tasty.* * *

* * * This morning the Pope summoned the Sacred College to his chamber to read the draft of his first encyclical. Entitled *De Lecto Conjugale*, it is concerned with the role of sexuality in marriage and related problems of birth control, world population problems *etcetera*. The Pope made moving reference to his own wife, who died in her fourth childbirth, and not a few of Their Eminences were to be observed surreptitiously wiping away a tear with the hems of their glowing robes. Scarlettofeverini, however, waxed more and more indignant as the reading proceeded, and could scarce restrain himself from bursting into protest. The Pope concluded by asserting that, in the present state of theological uncertainty, the practice of birth control by any method was left to the discretion and conscience of the Faithful. At the same time he called for the establishment of clinics in every parish to instruct married Catholics in all available techniques.

'This is paganism!' Scarlettofeverini erupted, when the Pope concluded. 'This is a return to paganism. This is the darkest day in the history of the Church since Luther nailed up his ninety-five theses.'

'On the contrary,' replied the Pope, 'We believe We have forestalled a second Reformation.'

'Luther would have been on your side today,' snarled the Cardinal, gathering the skirts of his robes preparatory to a stormy exit.

'Very likely,' said the Pope, with a smile. 'Luther was a married man.'

'I am the thirteenth child of my mother,' cried the angry prelate.

'And the father of none,' returned the Pope dryly.

Tee hee!

Today, after Vespers, Sister Maria asked me what is this birth control. I told her it did not concern her. Still, I suppose I must find out.* * *

* * * The impact of the new encyclical has been prodigious, despite attempts to have it banned in Sicily and Ireland. The Anglican Church has come over to Rome in a body. So many lapsed Catholics are returning to the practice of their Faith that the churches cannot accommodate them. *Gloria in excelsis Deo** * *

'Hallo, hallo, hallo! Dreaming again, Appleby?'

Adam relinquished his vision with regret, and looked up. 'Oh, hallo Camel,' he said.

Camel seated himself beside Adam, and pulled out his pipe. Adam said: 'Do you like cigars?'

'Why? Have you got one?'

Adam offered him one of the cigars the American had given him. Camel whistled.

'Where did you get this?'

'An American I helped out of a phone booth.'

'Sounds as if you've made a useful friend.'

'If I was the hero of one of these comic novels,' said Adam, 'he would be the fairy-godfather who would turn up at the end to offer me a job and a girl. Don't suppose I shall ever see him again, actually.'

'You never know.'

'Anyway, I've already got a girl. That's the whole trouble.'

'Still, you could use a job.'

'In America? It costs about five hundred pounds every time you have a baby, doesn't it?'

'Poor old Adam,' said Camel, drawing appreciatively on his cigar. 'You really are depressed, aren't you?'

'I don't see the point of my life at all,' said Adam. 'The only thing about it that seems really mine is sex – literature has annexed the rest. But sex is my big problem. I don't have enough of it, and when I do I get sick with worry. For two pins I'd buy twin beds and give myself up entirely to literature.'

'Don't do that,' said Camel.

'Then I think of people like Pond at it night after night, with text-books open for reference on the bedside table, and it just doesn't seem fair.'

'George is an awful liar,' said Camel. 'You mustn't believe all he tells you.'

'What d'you mean?'

'Would you like to hear the true story of his limp?'

'How do you know it?'

'Oh, it came out over a few more beers. In the pub, after you'd left.'

'You're a natural confessor, Camel,' said Adam. 'You should have been a priest.'

'Yes, I've often thought I'd enjoy shriving people,' mused Camel. 'That's why I started in psychology when I first came up to college. But I couldn't do the Maths.'

'So what's the true story of Pond's limp?' insisted Adam, his curiosity whetted.

Camel exhaled a long plume of blue smoke. The cool breeze off the forecourt blew it back in their faces, surrounding them in an aromatic haze and imparting a smoking-room atmosphere to the chilly, cloistral setting.

'Well, you know the Ponds have one child, Amanda?' Camel began.

'Yes.'

'For some time they have been considering having another.'

'Fools.'

'Have you not observed the unacceptibility of the only child in the contemporary middle-class ethos? Anyway, George and Sally decided to have a second child. But they don't want more than two.'

'I should think not.'

'It is particularly desirable, therefore, that the new infant should be of the male gender. Sally always wanted a boy. George is more concerned with the neatness of the arrangement. No point in duplicating, he says. Now, this is one problem modern science has so far failed to solve. But George, as we know, is as superstitious in sexual matters as he is rational in religious matters. It appears that when they were on holiday in Italy last summer they picked up a bit of local folklore to the effect that boys are conceived when the wife is full of desire and the husband fatigued and indifferent, and girls are conceived when the opposite circumstances prevail.'

'I should have thought it was the other way round,' said Adam.

'Quite. The formula has just enough unexpectedness to make it plausible,' Camel said. 'Apparently when Italian husbands wish to conceive a boy they visit a brothel before repairing to the matrimonial bed. George thought they ought to follow the prescription faithfully, but Sally wasn't having any of that. So they worked out an alternative scheme.

'The day for the experiment was determined by elaborate calculations performed with the aid of a calendar.'

'Good God,' Adam interrupted. 'D'you mean other people go through all that business?'

'On occasion,' Camel replied. 'The fateful day was a Sunday,' he went on. 'The idea was to get Sally feeling as sexy as possible and George feeling as exhausted as possible. George complained that it was a pity they hadn't known about the scheme before Amanda was conceived so that he could have had his turn at the better half of the deal, but he accepted his role manfully.

'All day long, Sally lounged about the house in a new negligée she had bought especially for the occasion, while poor old George sweated away in the garden, digging up flower-beds, mowing the lawn and trimming the hedges. At about six, he said that if they didn't go to bed soon he would fall asleep on his feet; but Sally persuaded him to wait another hour or two, and told him there was a lot of wood in the garden shed which needed chopping. Before she went upstairs to take a leisurely bath, Sally rooted in George's bookshelves for a sexy book to read in bed, and finally selected a Henry Miller, *Tropic of Capricorn* I think it was, which she'd heard was highly inflammatory.

'So, as dusk fell on West Norwood, and the neighbours settled comfortably before their television screens, Sally sat up in bed, bathed, perfumed and powdered, clad in a transparent black nightie, also bought for the occasion, reading Henry Miller; while, in the garden below, George, his hair matted, his shirt soaked with perspiration, furiously chopped wood, swearing occasionally as he nicked his fingers in the poor light.

'Then, curious things began to happen. Exhausted as he was, George found that the unwonted exercise and fresh air of the day had given him a feeling of health and vigour that he had not experienced for years. As he worked with demonic energy in the gathering dusk, the thought of Sally waiting for him upstairs, stretched out languorously on the four-poster bed in the warm, rosily lit bedroom, excited him. Even the rank odour rising from his own perspiring body gave him a strange feeling of brutal animal joy. He began to think they would have to change their plans. Still grasping his chopper, he entered the house with the intention of consulting Sally.

'Meanwhile, back at the boudoir, Sally had been having trouble with Henry Miller, whom she found emetic rather than erotic. Reading on and on with appalled fascination, she was filled with a deepening disgust for human sexuality. With a shock, she realized what was happening to her: she no longer had any inclination for intercourse that night. She threw down her book and jumped out of bed, determining to seek in George's library something more conducive to the arousal of passion – *Fanny Hill*, perhaps.

'Sally reached the head of the staircase just as George reached the foot. At the sight of her husband, tousled, dirty, breathing hard, wielding a chopper, Sally froze. For George, the spectacle of Sally, prettily discomposed, standing against the light in her black transparent nightie, was too much. Gone were all thoughts of conceiving children, male or female. George lunged up the stairs intent on nothing less than rape. With a faint scream, Sally fled to the bedroom, George hot in pursuit. Whether from exhaustion or excess of passion, however, he stumbled, tripped and fell to the bottom of the stairs, the chopper inflicting a slight flesh-wound on his thigh.'

'Hence the limp?'

'Hence the limp. Needless to say, no amorous dalliance took place that night. What makes George madder than anything, apparently, is all the wood he chopped. He'd completely forgotten that they had oil-fired central heating.'

Adam had ambivalent feelings about the story of Pond's limp. On the one hand, he was bitterly envious of those who enjoyed such confidence in the control of conception that they had reached the point of wanting to plan *sexes*; on the other, he took a certain heartless pleasure in the fact that those who had reached such refinements in the ordering of their sexual lives were not immune from humiliation and defeat. On balance, he had to acknowledge that Camel had managed to cheer him up, and he followed his friend into the Museum with almost a springy step. Unfortunately, he made the mistake of phoning Barbara again. She was a long time answering the phone.

'What is it now, Adam?' she asked wearily.

'Nothing, darling. I just thought I'd ring up and ask how you were feeling.'

'I'm feeling lousy.'

'Oh. No developments?'

'No. Mary Flynn has gone, and I'm lying down.'

'How was Mary?'

'She depressed me. First thing she said when she came to the door was, "Don't tell me: you're pregnant." '

'Oh my God. Why did she say that?'

'I don't know. She thinks she's pregnant again herself, so perhaps she was just trying to cheer herself up. Actually, we were both crying most of the time she was here.'

'But she must have had some reason for saying that.'

'There's a certain look in the eyes of women who think they're pregnant. No, two looks: the smug, happy look, and the desperate, unhappy look. I have the desperate, unhappy look.'

'So you do think you're pregnant, then?' said Adam miserably.

'I don't know, Adam. I don't know any more. I'm sick to death of the whole business.'

'Why don't you have a frog-test? Then at least we'd know where we stood. It's the waiting that gets you down.'

'Dr Johnson said last time he wouldn't prescribe any more tests – not on the National Health, anyway. Besides, by the time the result came through, I'd know anyway.'

Damn! damn! damn! With this unspoken expletive, Adam marked every step he took down the steep and dangerous stair-case that led to the Readers' lavatory. Camel had often told him how, some years before, this convenience had been closed for renovation, compelling scholars belatedly aware, as they rose from their desks to consult the catalogue, of full bladders, to walk a painful distance to the public lavatories in the main building. When the Readers' lavatory was open again, nothing seemed changed, except that the urinal had been raised on a marble plinth, thus ensuring the collision of the unwary head with the cisterns fixed to the wall. Camel had discovered, however, that this alteration could be turned to advantage: by resting one's forehead gently against the cistern while relieving oneself, a refreshing coolness was communicated to the aching brow. Adam now followed this procedure as he straddled his legs and unzipped his fly. His head needed soothing. Damn, damn, damn. Another child. It was unthinkable. Not all that again: sleepless nights, wind, sick; more nappies, more bottles, more cornflakes.

He had been fumbling unsuccessfully in his groin for some moments, and was beginning to suspect that he had been drugged and castrated at some earlier point in the day, when he remembered that he was wearing Barbara's pants. Hastily adjusting his dress, he retired to the privacy of a closet. Squatting there, his ankles shackled in nylon and lace, Adam wondered how they would accommodate another baby in the flat. It comprised only two rooms, plus kitchen and bathroom. One of the rooms had originally been a living-room, but this had long ago become Adam's and Barbara's bedroom, while the children occupied the other. This seemed the logical and inevitable design of a good Catholic home: no room for *living* in, only rooms for breeding, sleeping, eating and excreting. As it was, he was compelled to study in his bedroom, his desk squeezed up beside the double bed, constant reminder of birth, copulation and death. But what would happen now, for a new child could not be accommodated in the children's room? They would have to take it into their own room. Where, then, would he study? Perhaps he could sit in the bath, with a board across the top . . . But the taps dripped all the time. Besides, the bathroom was the busiest place in the house. They would have to move. But they couldn't move. Nowhere could they find a bigger flat in London at even double the price. He would have to leave home to make room for the incoming child. Not that he could afford separate accommodation, but perhaps he could live in the Museum, hiding when the closing bell rang and dossing down on one of the broad-topped desks with a pile of books for a pillow.

Damn, damn, damn. Adam plodded up the steep staircase, and returned to the Reading Room. He met the eye of the man behind the Inquiries desk, who gave him a smile of recognition. Inquiries he would like to make passed through Adam's head: where can I get a three-bedroomed flat at £3 10s od per week? What is the definition of a long sentence? Would you like to buy a second-hand scooter? What must I do to be saved? Adam returned the smile wanly and passed on.

He paused beside a shelf of reference books, and took down a rhyming dictionary.

I always buy a Brownlong chair . . .

Air, bare, bear, care, dare, e'er, fair, fare, glare, hair, hare, heir, lair, mare, pair, rare, scare, stair, stare, ware, wear, yare.

>It's just like floating in the air
>Another chair I couldn't bear
>And then I sit and stare and glare
>Like a lion in his lair
>Or a tortoise crossed with hare
>Or a horse without a mare
>Or a man who's got no heir
>Or an heir who's got no hair
>Hypocrite lecteur! Mon semblable, mon frère!

Adam replaced the rhyming dictionary, and moved on. Publish, Briggs had said, publish your piece on Merrymarsh. Little did he know it had already been rejected by nine periodicals. It was no use trying to publish criticism, unless you had a name, or friends. Discovering original materials was the only sure way. 'A Recently Discovered Letter of Shelley's'. 'Gerard Manley Hopkins's Laundry Bills'. 'The Baptismal Register at Inverness'. That was the sort of thing. Even unpublished manuscripts of Merrymarsh would do the trick, thought Adam, as he slumped into his seat before a heap of Lawrence.

At that moment he simultaneously remembered the strange-looking letter he had received that morning, and knew what it was about. He dug out the envelope, and feverishly tore it open. A rapid perusal of its contents confirmed his intuition.

Dear Mr Appleby,

Thank you very much for your letter. I am delighted to discover that there are still some young people in the world today who are concerned with the higher life, and still interested in the writings of dear Uncle Egbert. I have often tried to get my daughter to read his charming fantasies, like The Return of Piers Plowman and The Holy Well, but she is all too typical of the younger generation.

You ask if I have any unpublished manuscripts or letters of Uncle Egbert's. It so happens, I do have some papers of his which he gave me just before his death. I should think they would be of the greatest interest to a serious-minded young man like yourself. If you would like to see them I should be only too pleased.

Yours sincerely

Amy Rottingdean

The address at the head of the letter was in Bayswater.

Adam was flooded with excitement, and felt an urgent desire to communicate it. He gave Camel, who was dozing at the neighbouring desk, a nudge. Camel woke with a start.

'What is it?' he said crossly.

'I'm on the brink of a literary discovery,' whispered Adam. 'You remember months ago, when I was still working on Merry-marsh, I wrote to his publishers asking if there were any un-published Mss around?'

'I seem to recall something of the kind.'

'Well, they must have passed on the letter to the family, and I've had this letter from Merrymarsh's aunt, niece I mean. Look.'

He passed the letter, scrawled in green biro on black-edged mourning paper.

'She sounds a bit potty,' said Camel, handing back the letter. 'And I thought you'd lost interest in Merrymarsh.'

'Well, I've got it back now,' said Adam. 'Don't you see? There's bound to be something publishable here. Good for an article or two at the least. There might be some interesting letters. Merrymarsh was a hopeless writer, but he knew some good ones.'

Camel gave him an ironical glance. 'So you're going to chuck criticism and go in for scholarship?'

'Well, criticism hasn't got me anywhere,' said Adam defensively. He was prevented from continuing by signs of disapproval from neighbouring readers. His voice had been steadily rising in volume during the conversation. Adam returned to the silent perusal of his letter. Well, why not, he thought. Why not abandon his unfinished and unfinishable thesis, and start afresh on the letters of Egbert Merrymarsh? There was nothing very difficult about editing, was there? With luck he could finish the job by June and get his Ph.D. And then he would get it published. He saw the neat, slim volume in his mind's eye. *The Letters of Egbert Merrymarsh*, edited and with an introduction by Adam Appleby. It was the sort of thing the Sunday reviewers would fall on with cries of glee. 'Mr Appleby has performed a valuable service in bringing to light these documents of a vanished, but peculiarly fascinating corner of English literary life . . .'

Adam began to feel distinctly cheerful. Perhaps Barbara was not pregnant after all. Now he came to consider the matter calmly, it was obvious that she could not possibly be pregnant. How often in the past they had worried themselves into gloomy certainty that conception had taken place, only to be disproved, and how absurd it always seemed afterwards that they should have entertained any anxiety at all. Of course Barbara was not pregnant. He would ring her up and tell her so, at once. And tell her about the letter.

In the phone booth, Adam discovered that he had run out of change. He went to the postcard shop near the Elgin Marbles, and obtained a handful of threepenny bits at the cost of purchasing a sepia likeness of the British Museum. When he finally rang Barbara, however, there was no reply. Mrs Green was evidently out, and probably Barbara had taken the children to the park. Adam thought of his wife pushing their creaking, lopsided pram through the grey, damp afternoon in Battersea Park, past the ghost-town of the Fun Fair, closed for the winter, brooding on her possible pregnancy, and a pang of pity and love transfixed him. If only he could reach her, and assure her that all was well.

He returned to his desk in the Reading Room, but could not convert his good spirits into industry. The laboriously accumulated notes of his thesis filled him with impatience. That was all behind him now. Let the long sentence trail its way through English fiction as it willed – he would pursue it no longer. He took up Mrs Rottingdean's letter again, and began to draft a reply, asking if he could come round and see the papers as soon as possible, proposing the following evening. Yet he could scarcely contemplate the suspense of waiting even that long. Why should he not phone now, and propose calling on Mrs Rottingdean that very day? He looked again at the letter. Yes, a telephone number was given. Adam left his seat, and hurried back to the telephone.

As Adam pushed the door of the phone booth shut with his posterior and, trembling with excitement, dug in his pocket for change, a telephone bell rang, loud and insistent. Adam looked about him in bewilderment, unable to accept at first that the sound emanated from the instrument before him. But it evidently did. He lifted the receiver, and said hesitantly, 'Hallo.'

'Museum Double-O-One-Two?' demanded a female voice.

Adam obediently scrutinized the number at the centre of the dial. 'Yes,' he replied.

'Hold on please. Your call from Colorado.'

'What?' said Adam.

'Sorry it's taken so long, Museum,' said the operator brightly. 'The lines are absolutely haywire today.'

'I think you've got the wrong person,' Adam began. But the operator had gone away. Adam wanted to go away too, but didn't have the courage. Besides, he wanted to make a phone call himself. He opened the door of the kiosk and, still holding the receiver to his ear, leaned out to look into the foyer of the Museum, hoping to catch sight of the fat American.

'Are you there, Museum?'

'Oh. Yes, but look here –' Withdrawing his head too quickly, Adam banged it on the door and dropped the receiver, which swung clattering against the wall. By the time he recaptured it, the operator had gone again, and a faint American voice was saying anxiously:

'Bernie? Is that you, Bernie? Bernie?'

'No, it's not, I'm afraid,' said Adam.

'Ah, Bernie. I thought I'd lost you.'

'No, I'm not Bernie.'

'Who are you then?'

'My name's Appleby. Adam Appleby.'

'Pleased to make your acquaintance, Mr Appleby. Is Bernie there?'

'Well no, I'm afraid he isn't. I'm sorry you've had all this trouble and expense, but –'

'He's out, is he? Well, OK, you can give him a message. Will you tell him he can have one hundred thousand for books and fifty thousand for manuscripts?'

'One hundred thousand for books,' Adam repeated, mesmerized.

'Right. And fifty grand for manuscripts,' said the man. 'That's great, Adam, thanks a lot. You been working with Bernie for long?'

'Well, no,' said Adam. 'As a matter of fact –'

'Your time's up, Colorado,' said the operator. 'Do you want to pay for another two minutes?'

'No, that's all. 'Bye, Adam. Say hallo to Bernie for me.'

'Good-bye,' said Adam weakly. The line went dead.

Adam replaced the receiver and leaned against the door, wondering what he should do. He might never see the fat man again. He couldn't carry this undelivered message around with him for the rest of his life. It sounded important, too. A hundred thousand for books. Fifty grand for manuscripts. That meant dollars. Perhaps he should report the whole business to the operator.

Adam dialled 'O', and tried to rehearse a coherent explanation of the situation as he listened to the ringing tone.

'Is that the police?' a male voice inquired.

'Eh?' said Adam. He could still hear a ringing tone.

'My car has been stolen,' said the man. 'Would you please send an officer round at once?'

'You'd better dial 999,' said Adam. 'I'm not a policeman.'

'That's what I did dial,' said the man crossly.

'What number do you require?' said a third voice, female, sounding very faint. The ringing tone had stopped.

'I told you, I want the police,' said the man. 'Look here, my car has vanished. I haven't time to wait here while –'

'Are you there, caller?' said the operator.

'Do you mean me?' said Adam.

'Well, you dialled "O" didn't you?' inquired the operator, ironically.

'I keep telling you, I dialled 999,' screamed the man. 'What kind of a fool d'you take me for?'

'Yes, I dialled "O",' said Adam, dimly aware that he was the only member of the trio that enjoyed two-way communication with both the other parties.

'Well, what do you want then?' said the operator.

'I want the police,' sobbed the man.

'He wants the police,' explained Adam.

'You want the police?' asked the operator.

'No, I don't want the police,' said Adam.

'Where are you speaking from?' said the operator.

'Ninety-five Gower Street,' said the man.

'The British Museum,' said Adam. 'But I don't want the police. It's this other man who wants the police.'

'What is the name?'

'I don't know his name,' said Adam. 'What's your name?' he added, trying to throw his voice in the direction of Gower Street.

'Never mind my name,' said the operator, huffily. 'What's yours?'

'Brooks,' said the man.

'His name is Brooks,' Adam passed it on.

'Well, Mr Brooks –'

'No, no! My name is Appleby. Brooks is the man whose car was stolen.'

'You've had some books stolen, from the British Museum, is that it?' said the operator, as if all was clear at last.

'I've had enough of this foolery,' said Brooks angrily. 'But I assure you, I'm going to report it.' He slammed down his receiver. Adam registered his departure with relief.

'Look,' he said to the operator, 'are you the one who put through a call just now from Colorado for a man called Bernie?'

'Burning?' said the operator. 'You don't want the police, you need the fire service.'

Adam quietly replaced the receiver, and crept into the next booth. Essentially, he felt he had had enough of telephones for that day, but his anxiety to contact Mrs Rottingdean overcame his unwillingness to pick up the receiver again. Repeated dialling, however, elicited only a persistent engaged signal. Adam suspected that the line was out of order, but could not summon up the courage to ring the operator again. He tried ringing Barbara, but Mrs Green answered to say she was still out. Adam made one more unsuccessful attempt to ring Mrs Rottingdean, and retired, defeated and disgruntled, from the telephone. His excitement and enthusiasm were quite dissipated. He thought Barbara was probably pregnant after all.

6

Free or open access can hardly be practised in so large a library as this. As it was once put, the danger would be not merely of losing the books, but also of losing readers.

Arundell Esdaile (former secretary to the British Museum)

When Adam opened the door of the telephone booth, an unfamiliar and sacrilegious hubbub assaulted his ears. After he had taken a few paces it was the turn of his eyesight to be astonished. The main entrance hall was thronged with people chatting and gesticulating with an animation quite untypical of visitors to the Museum. They were held back on each side by a cordon of policemen, leaving open a narrow corridor extending from the revolving doors at the entrance to the Reading Room. Was it the Beatles again? Adam wondered. He pushed his way towards the entrance to the Reading Room, and showed his pass.

'Sorry, sir,' said the man. 'No one allowed in.'

'What's the matter?' said Adam.

The crowd raised an ironical cheer, and looking round Adam saw that the revolving doors were now fanning into the hall a steady stream of booted and helmeted firemen, who trotted sheepishly along the human corridor and into the Reading Room. Hosepipes snaked across the floor behind them.

'They say there's a fire,' said the doorman, with relish.

'Not in the Library?' exclaimed Adam, aghast.

'It's like the war all over again,' said the man, rubbing his hands together. 'Of course, most of the books are irreplaceable, you know.'

It wasn't, however (Adam had ashamedly to admit to himself later), the fate of the Museum's priceless collection which pre-occupied him at that moment, but the fate of his own notes and files. Only a short while ago he had been filled with disgust for that tatty collection of paper; but now that it was in danger of extinction he realized how closely his sense of personal identity, uncertain as this was, was involved in those fragile, vulnerable sheets, cards and notebooks, which even now might be crinkling and turning brown at the edges under the hot breath of destructive flame. Almost everything he had thought and read for the past two years was recorded there. It wasn't much, but it was all he had.

'Mind your back, sir,' said the doorman, as a fireman lumbered past. The hosepipe he was dragging by its nozzle caught under the door, and Adam sprang forward to disengage it. Clinging to the hosepipe, he trotted after the fireman.

'Hey!' called the doorman.

Adam ducked his head and kept trotting. It was only when he was inside the Reading Room and to his surprise and relief saw no evidence of conflagration, that he connected the presence of the firemen with his recent triangular conversation on the telephone. Then he wished he hadn't been in such a hurry to get into the Reading Room. He backed towards the door, but another official, more determined-looking than the first, told him sternly: 'Nobody allowed out yet, sir. There's no immediate danger.'

Adam believed him. But the other readers were not so confident. Clasping their notebooks to their breasts, as if the former were precious jewels snatched from the cabins of a foundering ship, they milled about the door begging to be let out. One lady tottered forward to the official and pressed a huge pile of typewritten sheets into his unwilling arms. 'I don't care about myself,' she said, weeping, 'but save my doctoral dissertation.'

Beyond the doorway, similar disorder prevailed. Some readers stood on their desks, and gazed about hopefully for rescue. Pushing his way through the crowd, Adam nearly tripped over a prostrate nun, saying her rosary. Near by, a Negro priest, hurriedly collecting his notes on St Thomas Aquinas, was being urged to hear someone's confession. A few courageous and stoical souls continued working calmly at their books, dedicated scholars to the last. One of them betrayed his inner tension by lighting a cigarette, evidently reasoning that normal fire precautions were now redundant. He was immediately drenched with chemical foam by an over-enthusiastic fireman. Shouts and cries violated the hallowed air which had hitherto been disturbed by nothing louder than the murmur of subdued conversation, or the occasional thump of dropped books. The dome seemed to look down with deep disapproval at the anarchic spectacle. Already ugly signs of looting were in evidence. Adam caught sight of a distinguished historian furtively filling the pockets of his raincoat from the open shelves.

Camel was sitting on his desk and surveying the scene with obvious enjoyment.

'Hallo, Appleby. I say, this is entertaining, isn't it?'

'Aren't you alarmed?'

'No, it's only some hoax.'

'A hoax, you think?'

'Bound to be. Shouldn't like to be the hoaxer when they catch him.'

Adam racked his brains to try and remember if he had given his name to that idiot operator. He rather feared that he had, but surely she wouldn't have got it right? He glanced guiltily over his shoulder, and looked straight into the eyes of a member of the Library staff who was standing near the catalogue shelves, supervising the loading of the huge volumes on to trolleys, by which means they were carted off to safety. The man's face registered recognition, and he began pushing his way towards Adam, waving a piece of paper.

'See you later,' said Adam to Camel.

As he shouldered his way through the panic-stricken crowd, tripping over trailing hosepipes, and stumbling over the backs of firemen who, on hands and knees, were searching under the desks for signs of fire, Adam cast fleeting glances over his shoulder. The assistant was talking to Camel, who was pointing in Adam's direction. Camel's idea of entertainment, he thought bitterly, as he reached the short passage which connected the Reading Room and the North Library.

He knew of no other way out of the North Library: if he went in, he would be trapped. He leaned against the wall at his back and pressed the palms of his hands against its surface. A soft, almost human warmth surprised his sense of touch. It wasn't a wall at all, but a door – a green baize door. His fingers found the handle and softly turned it. The door opened. He slipped through, and closed it behind him.

He was in another country: dark, musty, infernal. A maze of iron galleries, lined with books and connected by tortuous iron staircases, webbed his confused vision. He was in the stacks – he knew that – but it was difficult to connect this cramped and gloomy warren with the civilized spaciousness of the Reading Room. It was as if he had dropped suddenly from the even pavement of a quiet residential street into the city's sewers. He had crossed a frontier – there was no doubt of that; and already he felt himself entering into the invisible community of outcasts and malefactors – all those who were hunted through dark ways shunned by the innocent and the respectable. A few steps had brought him here, but it was a long way back. Never again would he be able to take his place beside the scholars in the Reading Room with a conscience as untroubled as theirs. They worked with a quiet confidence that wisdom was at their fingertips – that they had only to scribble on a form and knowledge was delivered promptly to their desks. But what did they know of this dark underworld, heavy with the odour of decaying paper, in which that knowledge was stored? Show me the happy scholar, he thought, and I will show you the bliss of ignorance.

Voices, sharp and authoritative, were raised on the other side of the door. He had a sudden vision of the capture, the indictment and the punishment, and stumbled blindly towards a flight of stairs. He grasped the bannister like salvation. If only I wasn't limping, he thought; but it was the treachery of Camel which stabbed more keenly than the pain in his leg.

The staircase spiralled up into darkness, like a fire escape in hell, fixed there to delude the damned. He dragged himself up four flights, and limped along a narrow gangway between tall shelves of books. He was in Theology. Abelard, Alcuin, Aquinas, Augustine. Augustine, the saint who knew sin from experience. He took down a volume in some vague hope of finding counsel in it, but was distracted by the sight of a cheese sandwich at the back of the shelf. It looked dry, and a little mouldy: the corners were turned up like the feet of a corpse. He thought he heard the scuttle of a mouse somewhere behind the books. It gave him a strange feeling of consolation to think that another human being – perhaps another fugitive – had passed through this cemetery of old controversies, and had left this mark of his passage.

Iron-shod feet rang on the iron grating. He felt the vibrations rise through the thin soles of his shoes, and through his bones and arteries, to knock at his heart. The hunt was on again.

He crept further along the shelving, past Bede and Bernard, Calvin and Chrysostom. A bundle of old tracts caught his eye. *Repent!* the cover of one admonished, *for the Day of Judgement is at Hand*. Another book bore the device of the Jansenist Christ, arms raised above the bowed head in a grim reminder of the exclusiveness of mercy.

Still the feet came on. A low moan broke from his lips as he turned to face his pursuer. Was this how the affair would end, then – trapped like an animal between walls of mouldering theology?

His hand groped instinctively for a weapon, but lighted only upon books: *A Quiverful of Arrows against Popery, Plucked from the Holy Scriptures* and *The Sin Against the Holy Ghost Finally Revealed.* Holding the two dusty volumes limply in his hands, he remembered the oozing wall of the urinal in the school playground, the tough Middle English paper in Finals, the fly-specked oleograph of the Sacred Heart in the Catholic doctor's waiting-room, and Barbara crying on the unmade bed; and the will to resist any longer ebbed out of him like water out of a sink, leaving behind only a sour scum of defeat. The footsteps paused, then came nearer. Twisting his head from side to side in the last throes of panic, he seemed to make out a few paces away the shape of a door, etched in thin cracks of light. He lunged towards it.

Adam realized his mistake as soon as he opened the door, but he had no choice but to proceed. He stepped across the threshold and closed the door behind him.

He had struggled through the entrails of the British Museum, only to come back to the womb again; but in an unfamiliar position. He was standing on the uppermost of the book-lined galleries that ran round the circular wall of the Reading Room beneath the dome. He had often idly watched, from his desk on the floors below, assistants fetching books from these shelves, and had admired the cunning design of the doors, whose inner surfaces were lined with false book spines so that when closed their presence could not be detected.

As a fugitive, he could scarcely have picked a more exposed and conspicuous refuge. Anyone who happened to glance up from the floor below would be sure to see him. Adam took a piece of paper from his pocket and shuffled along the shelves, pretending to be an assistant looking for books. He was painfully conscious of not wearing the regular overall, but it seemed as if there was sufficient commotion on the floor below to render him safe from observation. At length, lulled into a sense of security, and fascinated by the unfamiliar perspective in which he now viewed his place of work, Adam abandoned his pose and leaned on the gallery rail to look down.

Never before had he been so struck by the symmetry of the Reading Room's design. The disposition of the furniture, which at ground level created the effect of an irritating maze, now took on the beauty of an abstract geometrical relief – balanced, but just complicated enough to please and interest the eye. Two long counters extended from the North Library entrance to the centre of the perfectly circular room. These two lines inclined towards each other, but just as they were about to converge they swelled out to form a small circle, the hub of the Reading Room. Around this hub curved the concentric circles of the catalogue shelves, and from these circles the radii of the long desks extended almost to the perimeter of the huge space. A rectangular table was placed in each of the segments. It was like a diagram of something – a brain or a nervous system, and the foreshortened people moving about in irregular clusters were like blood corpuscles or molecules. This huge domed Reading Room was the cortex of the English-speaking races, he thought, with a certain awe. The memory of everything they had thought or imagined was stored here.

It seemed that the fire-alarm had been called off at last. The firemen were rolling up their hoses, or drifting out with wistful glances at the heavy furniture, fingering the hafts of their choppers. Disappointed journalists were being ushered firmly to the exit. A self-conscious group of readers was being interviewed by the BBC. At the counter for returned books there were long queues of people who had decided to call it a day. It was time he moved on, Adam felt.

He looked up, blinked and rubbed his eyes. Diametrically opposite him, and on the same level, the fat American was leaning on the rail of the gallery in the same attitude as himself, contemplating the animated scene below. Was he authorized to be there, Adam wondered; and, if so, was it safe for him to deliver his message? At that moment the American looked up, and seemed to see him. They stared at each other for several moments. Then Adam essayed a timid wave. The American responded with a nervous glance over his shoulder. It looked as though he had no more right to be there than Adam himself.

Adam began to walk round the circumference of the Reading Room anti-clockwise. The American responded by walking in the same direction. Adam halted and turned about. The American followed suit, keeping the same distance between himself and Adam. Adam wondered whether he could risk shouting his message across the intervening space, and decided he couldn't. Perhaps the gallery was a whispering one, he thought, with a certain pride in his resourcefulness; and pressing his cheek to Volumes IV and V of *The Decline and Fall of the Roman Empire*, he breathed the words, 'Colorado phoned.'

When he looked up to see if his message had carried, the American had disappeared. Adam hastened round the gallery to the point where he had last seen him, and explored the bookshelves with his fingertips, searching for the concealed door. He discovered it when it suddenly opened in his face, lightly grazing his nose and bringing tears to his eyes. An overalled assistant stood on the threshold.

'Excuse me,' Adam said, holding his nose to assuage the pain and mask his countenance. The man retired a couple of paces to let him pass, but eyed him suspiciously.

'What department are you in?' he demanded, adding hesitantly – 'sir.' The 'sir' gave Adam courage.

'Book-counting,' he said quickly. 'It's a new department.'

'Book-counting?' the man repeated, with a puzzled frown.

'That's right,' said Adam. 'We're counting the books.' He stepped briskly to the nearest shelf, and commenced running his index finger along the rows of books, muttering under his breath, 'Two million, three hundred thousand, four hundred and sixty-one, two million, three hundred thousand, four hundred and sixty-two, two million, three hundred thousand, four hundred and sixty-three . . .'

'You've got a job there,' said the man.

'Yes,' said Adam. 'And if you make me lose count, I'll have to start all over again from the beginning. Two million, three hundred thousand, four hundred . . .'

'Sorry,' said the man, humbly, and shuffled off towards the open door of the gallery. Adam poised himself to run; but the man hesitated at the door and returned.

'Sorry to disturb you again,' he said. 'But if you happen to find a sausage roll behind one of them books, you might let us know.'

'I found a cheese sandwich just now,' Adam offered. The man clapped a hand to his brow.

''Lord!' he exclaimed. 'I'd forgotten all about that cheese sandwich.'

When the man finally left him, Adam tiptoed away and scuttled down a narrow flight of stairs. He weaved his way through a labyrinth of bookshelves, hoping to stumble upon some way out. When he met anyone, he halted, and started counting books until they passed. At last he came upon a door from behind which he thought he could hear the sounds of ordinary human life. He slowly opened the door, and breathed a sigh of relief. He was at the North Entrance.

Fortunately for Adam, the North Entrance was thronged with a party of schoolgirls, and his furtive exit from the door marked 'Private' escaped the attention of the Museum attendants. On the other hand, when he had pulled the door shut behind him, he found he couldn't easily move. He began pushing his way through the scrum. Satchels poked him in the groin and hair got in his mouth. The girls giggled, or gave cries of indignation. Adam saw a mistress was observing him suspiciously, and his efforts to escape became frantic. All he needed now was to be arrested for indecent assault.

At last he was in the open air. He filled his lungs, and coughed. The fog was coming back. The end of Malet Street was invisible, and so were the top storeys of the Senate House tower. He turned to his right and began to circumnavigate the Museum. The trees of Russell Square loomed to his left like the vague shapes of drowned ships. He shivered and turned up the collar of his suit in a futile gesture of self-protection against the raw, damp air. His duffle coat was in the Reading Room, and he dared not return to recover it.

He had a vivid mental image of the duffle coat draped over the back of his padded chair, its hood drooping forward like the head of a scholar bowed over his books; and he not only coveted it but, in a strange way, almost envied it. It seemed like a ghost of his former self, or, rather, the external shell of the Adam Appleby who had, only a few days ago, been a reasonably contented man, but who now, haunted with the fear of an unwanted addition to his family, divided and distracted about his academic work, and guilty of a hoax he had had no intention of committing, wandered like an outcast through the foggy streets of Bloomsbury.

He turned into Great Russell Street, slippery with the last wet leaves of fall. A convoy of fire-engines roared through the gates of the Museum, and he shrank back against the railings as they passed. The Museum itself was shrouded in fog. Its windows were dim patches of light which shed no illumination on the bleak forecourt, deserted now except for a solitary taxi. Adam grasped the railings with both hands and pressed his cheeks against the chill, damp bars. Was it the fog or self-pity that made his eyes smart? He rubbed them with his knuckles, and immediately, as if the gesture had some magic property, he saw his wife and three children ascending the steps of the Museum. The atmosphere blurred the figures, but he could not mistake Barbara's baggy red coat, or Dominic's slack-limbed refusal to proceed, or the tilt of Clare's head, lifted to her mother in interrogation. As in a dream he watched Barbara, encumbered by the weight of Edward in her arms, stoop to plead with Dominic for cooperation. And it *was* a dream, of course. Although the Museum was notoriously a place where eventually you met everyone you knew, this law did not include dependants. Scholarship and domesticity were opposed worlds, whose common frontier was marked by the Museum railings. This reversal of the natural order, with himself outside the railings, and his family inside, was a vision, pregnant with symbolic significance if only he could penetrate it. He felt moved but helpless, like Scrooge watching the tableaux unfolded by the spirits of Christmas. He longed to run forward and help his wife, but knew that if he stirred a muscle the vision would dissolve. Sure enough, as he released his grasp on the railings and moved towards the gates, a puff of wind stirred the fog, and threw an impenetrable screen between himself and the steps. When it cleared partially, the steps were deserted again.

Still puzzled by the vividness and particularity of the apparition, Adam hurried through the gates and up the steps. He peered through the glass doors, but could see no sign of Barbara. Further he dared not go – the man at the entrance to the Reading Room was on the watch. He was distracted by the sound of children chasing pigeons somewhere to his left. The whoops and cries echoing faintly in the colonnade, mingled with the indignant commotion of wings, could be Dominic's. Adam hurried to investigate, but the children were not his own.

He drank some water at the stone fount near the doors of the Museum, pursing his lips and sucking noisily to avoid touching the lip of the battered metal cup. Then he paced up and down the colonnade, wondering what to do. The Reading Room would be open late that evening, he reminded himself. If he sneaked in towards closing time the fire alarm might have been forgotten, and he might be able to retrieve his belongings without notice. But what could he do in the meantime? There was the sherry party at six – that would take care of the early evening – but it was only three-thirty now.

Adam toyed with the idea of going to a cinema. He had a keen premonition of the guilt he would feel at adding a further act of idleness to a day already characterized by total non-achievement. But, on the other hand, was it any use fighting destiny? He rooted in his pockets to see how much money he had, and pulled out Mrs Rottingdean's letter. That was a thought. Suppose he took a chance – there would be no more telephoning – and went straight to her house? He might yet snatch something useful out of the day . . .

As he prepared to push-start his scooter, Adam quailed inwardly at the prospect before him. He was not experienced in negotiating for unpublished literary remains, but he knew that the relatives of deceased authors were liable to be touchy and obstructive in such matters. In any case he anticipated all new human contacts with fear and reluctance. He glanced wistfully at the Museum, but its dim, forbidding shape only reminded him how irretrievably he was committed to a career of risk. With stoic resolution he turned back to his scooter, and began to push it with increasing momentum between the lines of parked cars. He was going to need both courage and subtlety to succeed in his enterprise.

7

During the autumn and winter the delivery of a book is not
infrequently hindered by darkness or fog.

A Guide to the Use of the Reading Room (1924)

In the late afternoon the Museum was still there, but he was not
going to it any more. It was foggy in London that afternoon and
the dark came very early. Then the shops turned their lights on,
and it was all right riding down Oxford Street looking in the
windows, though you couldn't see much because of the fog.
There was much traffic on the roads and the drivers couldn't see
where they were going. The traffic lights changed from red to
amber to green and back to red again and the traffic didn't move.
Then the drivers sounded their horns and got out of their cars
to swear at each other. It was foggy in London that afternoon
and the dark came very early.

The house in Bayswater looked on to a square. There was
a playground in the square and some big trees. The swings in
the playground squeaked but you couldn't see the children who
were swinging because of the trees and the fog. It was a tall
narrow house and it hadn't been painted for a long time. The
old paint had flaked off in places and underneath you could see
the raw brickwork. There were six steps leading up to the front
door and more steps leading down to a basement area.

Adam knocked on the front door but it was the basement
door which opened. A man wearing a dirty vest and with a lot
of thick black hair on his arms and chest looked up.

'Mrs Rottingdean?' Adam said.

'Out,' the man said.

'Do you know when she'll be back?'

'No,' the man said, and shut the door.

Adam stood on the top step for a while, listening to the squeak of the swings in the square. Then he went down the area steps and knocked on the door of the basement.

'Come in,' the man said. He held the door open with his left hand and Adam saw that two fingers were missing from it.

'I just wanted to leave a message.'

'I said, "Come in".'

Adam went in. It was a large bare kitchen. There were some wooden chairs and a table and a lot of empty beer bottles in one corner. On the walls were some bull-fighting posters. The bulls were painted to look very fierce and the bullfighters to look very handsome. Two men sat at the table drinking beer and talking to each other in a foreign language. They were not very handsome and when they saw Adam they stopped talking. Adam looked at the bull-fighting posters.

'You are *aficionado*?' the hairy man said.

'I beg your pardon?'

'You follow the bulls?'

'I've never been to a bull-fight.'

'Who is he?' one of the men at the table said. The thumb was missing from his left hand.

'Who are you?' the hairy man said to Adam.

'He's from the café,' the third man said. This man's left hand was in a sling.

'There must be some mistake,' Adam said.

'I'll say there is,' the man with the sling said. 'We just called the café.'

'I haven't come from any café,' Adam said. 'I've come from the British Museum.'

'They have a café there?'

'They call it a cafeteria,' Adam said.

'Same thing,' the man with the sling said.

'That is not so,' the man with one thumb missing said. 'A café is a place where a man may drink with his friends and the drinks are brought to him on a tray by a waiter. A cafeteria is a place for people who should have been waiters themselves, for there you carry your own tray. Also in a café you may drink beer or maybe wine. In a cafeteria only coffee or tea.'

'In this country you can drink only tea, wherever you go,' said the man with his arm in a sling. He put the neck of a beer bottle between his teeth and pulled off the metal cap. He spat out the cap and it rolled across the floor to Adam's feet. Adam picked up the cap and placed it on the table.

'Keep it,' the man with the sling said.

'Pay no attention to him,' the man with one thumb said. 'His hand hurts and he has no aspirins. You have some aspirins?'

'No,' Adam said.

'It is of no importance. It is only a small pain.'

'What you do in this Museum, then?' the hairy man said.

'He goes to the cafeteria to drink the tea,' the man with the sling said.

'Shuddup,' the hairy man said.

'I read books in the library there,' Adam said.

The man with only one thumb jerked it towards the ceiling. 'She has a lotta books,' he said.

'Mrs Rottingdean?' Adam said. 'It's her I wanted to see.'

'She's out,' the man with one thumb said.

'I told him that,' the hairy man said.

'I'll come back later,' Adam said.

'You wait here,' the hairy man said. He pulled up a chair for Adam. Adam sat down slowly.

At the other end of the kitchen a door opened and the figure of a young girl appeared. She had a white face and black hair and her dress was black.

'What do you want?' said the hairy man, without looking round.

'Nothing. Who is that?' the girl said, looking at Adam.

'He's from the café,' the man with the sling said. 'You got any aspirins?'

'No, you've used them all,' the girl said.

'Then get outta here.'

The door closed.

'Bad lot,' the man with the sling said.

'I think I'll be going,' Adam said, getting to his feet.

The hairy man pushed him down with a firm pressure on his shoulder. 'You wait here,' he said.

'So you read books?' the man with the sling said to Adam.

'Yes,' Adam said.

'What kind of books? Love stories?'

'Some of them are love stories.'

'I like a good movie myself,' the hairy man said.

'He is in love with Elizabeth Taylor,' the man with one thumb said.

The hairy man blushed and twisted one leg round the other. 'She is a magnificent woman,' he muttered.

'He has seen *Cleopatra* thirty-four times,' the man with one thumb said. 'Do you think that is a record?'

'I'm sure it must be,' Adam said.

'It is not. The girls who show the seat have seen it more often.'

The man with his arm in a sling choked on his beer bottle. The beer streamed down his chin and throat and soaked his vest. 'One day you will kill me, *amigo*,' he said.

'One day I will kill Richard Burton,' the hairy man said.

'Have you any idea when Mrs Rottingdean will be back?' Adam said.

'Richard Burton would not let you,' the man with the sling said. 'I have seen him knock down bigger men than you.'

'He is no bigger than yourself,' the hairy man said.

'I believe it.'

'I have knocked down many men your size,' the hairy man said. 'I would show you but your hand is in a sling.'

'Do you not understand in the movies it is all faked?' the man with one thumb said. 'It is not Richard Burton who knocks down or is knocked down. They are like children,' he said to Adam.

'I still have one good arm,' the man with the sling said. He thumped his elbow on the table and held his forearm vertically in the air. The hairy man sat down on the other side of the table and did the same, entwining the other's fingers in his own.

'Have it your own way,' the man with one thumb said. He opened another bottle of beer.

The two men struggled to force down each other's arms on to the table. The sinews on their bare forearms stood out in hard relief. Sweat poured from their foreheads, and formed dark patches under their armpits. The third man encouraged their efforts with a low, guttural crooning.

Adam got up from his seat and walked quietly to the door.

'Where are you going?' the man with one thumb said. The two men at the table stopped struggling and looked at him.

'I was looking for the lavatory,' Adam said.

'Through there.' The thumb gestured to the door at the other end of the kitchen.

It was a long walk between the two doors.

Adam opened and banged shut the door of the lavatory without going in. He did not want to use the lavatory. He did not want to wait for Mrs Rottingdean, supposing she existed. He just wanted to get out of the house and ride away into the fog, while he still had all his fingers. He had seen, in a film somewhere, that trial-of-strength game played with knives on the table.

A dark staircase led upwards from the basement. Adam felt his way cautiously up the stairs until his groping hands encountered a door. It yielded to a turn of the handle and Adam stepped into a carpeted hall. His first action was to close the door softly behind him. A hand-written notice on the door said, 'Keep Locked', and Adam was glad to obey: the key was in the lock. No doubt the girl he had seen in the kitchen had omitted to lock the door when she retreated. He blessed her for her forgetfulness.

He stood with his back to the door for a few moments, taking stock of his surroundings. The hall was dark and a little dingy. There was a large, heavy coatstand, and a grandfather clock with a ponderous, doleful tick. The walls were hung with large pictures of martyrs in various forms of agony: he identified St Sebastian transfixed with arrows like a pincushion, and St Lawrence broiling patiently on a grid-iron. While those morbid icons were consistent with what he knew of Mrs Rottingdean's religious background, they made him feel uncomfortable. He shrank from them as from something cruel and sinister. This will teach you to go whoring after unpublished manuscripts, he told himself. Don't you wish you were snug in the British Museum, counting the words in long sentences? Or at home dandling your three lovely children on your knee – knees?

Apart from the ticking of the clock, the house seemed quite silent and deserted. There was nothing to stop him from walking down the narrow strip of threadbare carpet, opening the front door, and leaping down the steps to his scooter. Nothing except the staircase at his right, to which his back would be exposed as he walked down the hall, and the three doors to his left, any one of which might open as he passed.

Then, suddenly, he heard the sound of music – pop music. It was faint, very distant, and he couldn't be sure whether it was carrying from some remote part of the house, or from outside. But its intimations of cheerful normalcy reassured him, and gave him courage to walk down the hall. He passed the doors to his left, one, two, three, without incident. A glance over his shoulder assured him that the stairs were unoccupied. His fingers reached out eagerly to grasp the latch of the heavy front door, and he pulled it open.

A large, middle-aged woman stood on the threshold pointing something at his chest. Adam raised his arms in surrender but checked himself as he saw it was only a Yale key.

'Who are you?' said the woman.

'Appleby – Adam Appleby,' he gabbled.

The woman regarded him through narrowed eyes. 'That rings a faint bell.'

'You must be Mrs Rottingdean . . .'

'Yes.'

'I wrote you a letter, and you wrote me one back. About Egbert Merrymarsh.'

'Oh yes,' said Mrs Rottingdean. 'May I come in?'

Adam stepped aside to let her pass. 'You must be wondering what I'm doing in your house . . .'

'I suppose my daughter let you in?'

'No, some men downstairs –'

'It's very bad of her. I've told her never to answer the door when I'm out.'

'No, she didn't really. These men –'

'Well, you're here anyway,' said Mrs Rottingdean, who seemed to be a little deaf. 'Won't you have some holy water?'

'I'm not thirsty, thanks.'

'I see you're not a co-religionist, Mr Appleby,' said Mrs Rottingdean, dipping her hand into a holy water stoup fixed to the wall, and crossing herself.

'Oh yes, I am,' said Adam. 'I just didn't understand . . .'

'If you'd like to sit down in here,' said Mrs Rottingdean, throwing open the door of a sitting-room, 'I'll make tea.'

The sitting-room was furnished much like the hall, with heavy, antiquated furniture and sombre religious paintings on the walls. There was a quantity of religious bric-à-brac on all the surfaces. Adam sat on the edge of a hard upright chair. He thought he heard someone pass the door which Mrs Rottingdean had closed behind him, and a few moments later he heard voices, faintly from the back of the house, but raised in anger. It sounded like Mrs Rottingdean and her daughter.

He got to his feet and prowled restlessly about the room. A human finger-bone under a glass case on the mantelpiece caused him a momentary twinge of fear: he wondered whether it had been donated by one of the troglodytes below. But a legend on the case read, 'Blessed Oliver Plunkett, Pray for us'. He went to the window and drew back the net curtains. It was quite dark outside and the street lamps glowed dully, each in an aureole of fog. The squat shape of his scooter was just visible at the kerb. That was all right, then. He turned back into the room and investigated a glass-fronted bookcase. It was locked, but he made out the titles of several of Merrymarsh's books, and other Catholic works of yesteryear: Chesterton's *The Napoleon of Notting Hill*, Belloc's *The Path to Rome*, Henry Harland's *The Cardinal's Snuff Box*, Robert Hugh Benson's *Come Rack! Come Rope!*, the *Poems* of John Gray. They looked like first editions, and he wondered whether they were autographed. A faint quiver of curiosity and excitement revived in him. In particular he was intrigued by a black box-file on the lowest shelf of the bookcase. On the faded label he could just make out the words, 'E.M. – Unpublished MS.'. Perhaps it was a good thing he had come after all. He resolved to make an impression on Mrs Rottingdean.

It was with a, for him, unwonted alacrity that our friend, hearing the tinkle of china in the hall, sprang gallantly to the door.

'I've been admiring your "things",' he said, as he assisted her with the tea-trolley.

'They're mostly my uncle's,' she said. 'But one does one's best.' She gestured vaguely to a cabinet where reliquaries, statuettes and vials of Lourdes water were ranged on shelves, dim dusty devotional.

She made tea in the old, leisured way, pouring the water into the pot from a hissing brass urn.

'One lump or . . .?' she questioned.

Weighing his reply, he had time to take stock of his new friend. She wore a simple robe of soft dark material, and shoes that, diffident as he was in such matters, he would not have felt altogether out on a limb in describing as 'sensible'. A plain gold cross at her bosom was her only ornament. Her countenance, innocent of paint, was regular, reposed, righteous – the kind of face he had glimpsed a hundred times in the gloom of cathedral side-chapels, pale above pale hands knotted in beads. She met his apprehension of her like the feel of a fine old missal in the palm: clean but well-thumbed, its cover softened by use but the spine still firm and straight.

'Two,' he said boldly.

'You have a sweet tooth,' she passed it off.

But he kept her to it. 'You are very perceptive.'

'Uncle Egbert had a sweet tooth,' she went on. 'He had a weakness for chocolate éclairs after Benediction on Sundays.'

'You lived with your uncle, then?'

For some reason the question seemed to disturb her, and she fumbled with the teaspoons.

'That was a long time ago,' she said.

The memory of Merrymarsh was evidently a tender one, and it seemed as though the question of manuscripts would have to be delicately broached. He fairly rattled the small change of conversation in his pocket without lighting on a single coin that wouldn't, in the circumstances, seem too soiled and worn, too vulgarly confident of being 'hard' currency.

'Won't your daughter be joining us?' he risked at last.

The shrewd grey eyes took it in. 'She has a headache. I hope you may have another opportunity of meeting her.'

'I hope so, too,' his answer was prompt.

'Perhaps you could explain her to me, Mr Appleby. I confess I don't understand the young people of today.'

Well, he had pressed a button of sorts, at all events.

'No doubt your own mother said the same of you, once,' he ventured with a smile.

Mrs Rottingdean put down her teacup. 'Between a Catholic mother and her daughter there should be no distrust.' She seemed to square him up in the vice of this statement before tapping home her next remark: 'Are you a *practising* Catholic, Mr Appleby?'

He was caught off balance, he couldn't disguise it. She dropped her eyes and murmured, 'I apologize. One should not ask such questions.'

'Oh, I don't mind admitting it to *you*,' he reassured her, with a rueful laugh.

'You mean . . .?'

'I mean there are occasions when, coward that one is, one prefers to let people think the worst. It is the homage virtue pays to vice.'

'Ah,' was all she had to say.

He put down his teacup.

'May I give you another?'

'Please. It is delicious.'

She poured expertly, from a height. 'Virginia has had a strict upbringing. Perhaps too strict. But I have old-fashioned ideas about girls' education.'

'Virginia.' He tested the ring of it. 'That is a charming name.'

Mrs Rottingdean looked him straight in the eyes. 'She will have two thousand pounds on marriage,' she said.

That was it, then. They had touched bottom at last; and like most bottoms it was muddy and a shade disillusioning, littered with the pathetic shapes of old broken things – prams, kettles and bicycle wheels. But he had to admire, as he shot back to the surface with bubbles trailing from his mouth in the form of a gay, 'Then I envy the bachelors of your acquaintance,' the brave effort with which, gasping only a little, she quickly rejoined him in the thinner element of polite conversation.

'You are married? And so young?'

'With three young children,' he rubbed it in. 'Which makes me all the more anxious, dear lady,' he went on, 'to make my fame and fortune with your generous assistance.'

'Oh, I am to be generous, am I?' she teased him.

'To a fault.'

'Ah, that is what I am afraid of.'

'How could you blame me for thinking so, after your kind letter?'

'Oh, *letters!*' Her emphasis was expressive.

'Quite. Letters,' he echoed, glancing involuntarily at the bookcase. Her eyes followed his, and they communed in silence. It took on quite a character of its own in the end, this silence, shaped by the consciousness they both had of the manifold things they, all understandingly, were *not* saying to each other.

'And if I hadn't written . . .?' she said at last.

'Oh, in *that* case . . .' His shrug conveyed, he hoped, the direness of such a hypothesis.

'You would have renounced all hopes of fame and fortune?'

'Well, no,' he admitted. 'But one must have materials.'

Mrs Rottingdean poured herself a second cup of tea and slowly stirred the cream into it. 'And what do you do with "materials" when you get them?'

'Read them, first. Then, if, as one always hopes, they turn out to be of interest, write about them. Perhaps even publish them.'

'And what are your criteria of "interest"?'

It was his turn to drop into directness. 'Well, I can't for instance imagine that anything that threw light on Egbert Merrymarsh and his circle would lack that quality.'

He leaned back in his chair and crossed his legs with a

casualness that was not altogether unstudied. Mrs Rottingdean scrutinized him for a moment, then rose to her feet. She took a key from the mantelpiece and went to the bookcase. She returned with the black box-file, which she placed on his lap.

'There you are, Mr Appleby,' she said. 'That contains all the unpublished writings of my uncle that I possess. You can have them for two hundred and fifty pounds. I won't take a penny less.'

Adam sat dejectedly in his chair, a thick manuscript open on his lap. He had long since abandoned reading it. From time to time the sum of money Mrs Rottingdean had mentioned returned to his mind and forced an incredulous snort of derision from his nostrils.

The black box-file had proved to contain a single bulky manuscript and a sheaf of letters from publishers explaining, with various degrees of rudeness, that they could not undertake publication. On the bottom of one of these letters, from a respectable Catholic house, was a note in Merrymarsh's sprawling hand: *More evidence of the Jewish-Masonic conspiracy against my work.*

The manuscript itself was a full-length book entitled *Lay Sermons and Private Prayers.* Adam had got as far as the sermon on Purity.

'When I was a lad at school,' it began,

we were taught religious instruction by a holy old priest called Father Bonaventure. Father Bonaventure wasn't the greatest theologian in Christendom; but he knew his catechism and he had a great devotion to Our Lady, and that was worth a thousand arguments to our young, unformed minds.

He based his moral instruction on the Ten Commandments, which he went through one by one. But when he reached the Sixth, 'Thou shalt not commit adultery,' he would say, 'I'll deal with that when I come to the Ninth Commandment.' And when he came to the Ninth, 'Thou shalt not covet thy neighbour's wife,' he would say, 'I'll deal with that when I come back to the Sixth Commandment.'

Some of the boys used to laugh at Father Bonaventure on this account; but it seems to me now, looking back gratefully to my schooldays, that old Father Bonaventure gave us the best instruction on purity that was ever given. For what was his artless evasion of the Sixth and Ninth Commandments but purity in action? And to speak the truth, there were few boys in that class, even among those who laughed at their old teacher, who were not secretly relieved that purity, the shyest and tenderest of virtues, was not dragged roughly out into the arena of public discussion.

We were, no doubt, a rough and ready set of fellows. Our collars were not always clean, our prep was not always faultless, and we were not over-scrupulous in respecting the rights of private property, particularly where apple orchards were concerned. But on one score we needed no correction; and if a newcomer to the school let a smutty word fall from his lips, or a lewd book from his pocket, he was soundly kicked for his pains, and was all the better for it. Talk about purity, it might be said at the risk of appearing paradoxical, begets impurity. It puts ideas into young heads which they would be better without. And after all, the talk is unnecessary. No one in his right body needs to be told that short skirts and mixed bathing are an offence against purity; not to mention the novels of Mr Lawrence, the plays of Mr Shaw, or the pamphlets of Dr Stopes in which the modern ideal of the Unholy Family is so graphically adumbrated . . .

At the end of the sermon, as at the end of all the other pieces in the book, was a rhymed prayer:

> You who made us pure as children
>> Keep us pure in adulthood.
> Let the beauty of creation
>> Be not a snare but source of good . . .

It was at this point that Adam had stopped reading. He tried to cheer himself up by entertaining some impure thoughts, but the circumstances were not congenial. He was locked in the room for one thing, and it made him restive. 'You won't mind me taking this precaution, will you?' Mrs Rottingdean had told, rather than asked him when she left him alone with the manuscript. 'I have to go out, and I don't believe in taking risks with valuable literary documents.' Valuable! No one in their senses would give two hundred and fifty pence for this garbage. One or two of Merrymarsh's books had a certain period charm, a vein of puckish whimsy. But this . . .

He looked at his watch: a quarter past five. If Mrs Rottingdean did not return soon he would be late for the sherry party. He went to the window and pushed experimentally at the sash, but it was stuck. In any case it was a long drop down to the area, and he had no desire to leave by that route.

He heard footsteps in the hall and scuttled back to his seat. As the key turned in the lock he picked up the manuscript and rehearsed the polite speech in which he planned to return the manuscript to its owner and excuse himself from lingering any longer in the house. But the person who entered was not Mrs Rottingdean. It was the girl he had glimpsed in the kitchen.

'Hallo,' she said.

'Hallo,' said Adam.

The girl leaned against the door and appraised him with a slow, sensual smile. She looked about nineteen, but was probably younger. She was pretty in a pale, neglected kind of way, and her figure, eloquently revealed by a black vee-necked sweater and tight skirt, was agreeably contoured.

'Do you know who I am?' she said.

'You must be Virginia.'

The girl sat down on a sofa opposite Adam and crossed her legs. 'D'you happen to have a cigarette?'

'Sorry. I don't smoke.' Something made him add, as if in mitigation, 'I gave it up.'

'Scared of cancer?'

'No, I just couldn't afford it.'

'What did Mother tell you about me?'

'Nothing much.'

'She thinks I'm wild and ungovernable. What's your name?'

'Adam.'

'D'you think I have nice breasts, Adam?'

'Yes,' he said truthfully.

'You can touch them if you like.' She patted the sofa invitingly.

Adam swallowed. 'I see what your mother means.'

Virginia giggled. 'What did she lock you up for? She's a great one for locking people up.'

'I don't really know. But since you've so kindly released me . . .' He stood up and glanced at his watch.

'Oh, don't go!'

'I'm afraid I must.'

Virginia danced to the door, locked it on the inside, and slipped the key inside the neck of her sweater. Then she resumed her place on the sofa, tucking up her legs. Adam sat down again.

'What did you do that for?'

'Can't you guess?'

'I'd rather not.'

Virginia uncoiled her legs and stretched out languorously on the sofa. 'I'm determined to seduce you, so you might as well resign yourself.'

'Please open the door,' he begged. 'Your mother may come back at any moment.'

Virginia shot him an eager glance. 'Is that your only objection?'

'Of course it isn't. For one thing, I have a wife and three children.'

'Good,' said Virginia. 'I like experienced men.'

Adam got up and tried the window sash again. 'It doesn't open,' said Virginia. 'Why did you come here?'

'You may well ask,' said Adam. 'Originally it was because I was interested in the writings of your great-uncle.'

Virginia wrinkled her brow. 'Great-uncle?'

'Your mother's Uncle Egbert.'

'Oh, Egbert Merrymarsh! Mother's lover. Did she tell you he was her uncle?'

'Your mother's *what*?'

'Mother's lover. He seduced her when she was twenty. That's why she's been so strict with me.'

Adam laughed.

'No, cross my heart, it's true.'

'And I suppose you're the illegitimate daughter. How romantic!'

''Course not, silly. He died years before I was born.'

Adam stood over the recumbent girl and stared into her eyes. They were like pools of black coffee, dark but transparent, and they did not waver. 'You're a good actress,' he said at last. 'If I hadn't been reading one of Merrymarsh's books for the last half-hour, I might have been taken in.'

'What have you been reading, then?'

He prodded the manuscript, which was lying on the floor, with his toe. 'This. *Lay Sermons and Private Prayers*.'

'Oh, *that* tripe.'

'Have you read it?'

'She tried to make me, once. *I* could show you something really interesting by him.'

'What?'

'Something *really* interesting.' She chuckled and wriggled her bottom in the sofa cushions.

He turned away. 'I've lost all interest in Merrymarsh anyway.' He went to the door and tested the lock. It was firm.

'Does your wife have frequent orgasms?' said Virginia.

'That's none of your business.'

'You're blushing. Don't you believe in the frank discussion of sex?'

'If you must know,' he said in exasperation, 'we don't have frequent intercourse.'

'But that's awful! Don't you love her any more?'

'We happen to be Catholics, that's all.'

'You mean you believe all that nonsense about birth control?'

'I'm not sure I believe it, but I practise it. Look, are you going to let me out, or aren't you?'

'You've only got to take the key.'

Setting his countenance grimly, he strode across the floor to the couch, and, with a gesture as brusque and clinical as he could manage, inserted his hand under Virginia's sweater. She did not flinch, but Adam did when he discovered that she was not wearing a brassiere. He withdrew his keyless hand, going hot and cold by turns. 'You've moved it,' he accused her.

'You have nice soft hands, Adam,' she said.

'Please give me the key. Aren't you afraid of what your mother will say when she comes back and finds you locked in here with me?'

'No. I have a hold over her because I know her past.'

Adam paced about the room. If only he could trip her up in some part of this ridiculous story, he felt, he might be able to bully her into letting him out.

'If that's the case, why don't you leave home – since you evidently don't see eye to eye with your mother?'

'She has a hold over *me*. She has some money in trust for me if I marry with her consent.'

'From Egbert Merrymarsh?'

'No, how could it be, silly? From my father. He died about ten years ago.'

Adam sat down. She was beginning to convince him, and a treacherous pulse of excitement and curiosity began to beat again at the back of his mind. He scented a scandal that would send a gratifying shock through certain quarters of the Catholic and literary worlds.

'Supposing all this about your mother's past is true, how did you discover it?'

'I found some letters from Merrymarsh to Mother. They're very passionate. She must have been a different person.'

'How old was Merrymarsh then?'

'I don't know. Quite old – about forty-five, maybe even more. Would you believe it – he was a virgin until then.'

'Are these letters the "something interesting" you mentioned just now?'

'No, I meant the book.'

'The book?'

'Yes, there was a book – in handwriting, you know, not a proper book. One day I saw Mother burning a lot of papers in the cellar, and while her back was turned I managed to salvage the book and a bundle of letters.'

'What kind of book is it?'

'Well, it's a sort of novel, written like a journal. It's really the story of his affair with Mother, with just the names changed. It's hot stuff, as we used to say at school.'

'Hot stuff?'

'It doesn't leave anything to the imagination,' said Virginia, with a leer.

'This is fantastic,' said Adam. 'Can I see the book?'

Virginia pondered, then shook her head. 'Not now, Mother will be back at any minute. Can you come back later tonight?'

'Just a quick glance,' he urged.

She shook her head again. 'No, I've hidden it, and it'll take some time to get out. Besides, I'm not going to all this trouble for nothing, Adam.' She extruded the tip of a pink, kittenish tongue and moistened her lips suggestively.

'Oh,' said Adam.

Simultaneously they became aware of an engine throbbing in the street outside.

'That's Mother's taxi,' said Virginia, jumping up.

'Oh God,' said Adam, following suit.

Virginia slipped a hand down the front of her skirt and produced the key. 'Next time you'll know where to look.' She went to the door and unlocked it. 'I'll have to lock you in again. See you tonight.'

'But how shall I manage it?'

'That's your problem, Adam.'

He tugged at her sleeve. 'Before you go – there's one question I must ask you. Who are those men downstairs?'

'Butchers,' was the cryptic reply. She slipped through the door, and he heard the key turn in the lock.

8

... studious and curious persons ...

Users of the British Museum, as defined by the Act of 1753

You who made us pure as children
Keep us pure in adulthood ...

Adam, driving blind through the fog, twisted the throttle of his scooter to try and drown the syllables which droned with maddening persistence in his head. The machine shuddered and lurched forward, adding a generous quota of fumes to the already foul atmosphere. The noise was satisfactory, but the speed perilous. He swerved violently to avoid a lorry abandoned by its driver. A little later a bone-shaking bump informed him that he had been travelling on the pavement. He overtook a line of cars following each other's tail lights at a crawl, and exchanged startled glances with the policeman who was leading the caravan on a motorcycle.

Let the beauty of creation
Be not a snare but source of good.

It was no use. He eased back the throttle and chugged at a more sedate speed down what he hoped was the Edgware Road.

He did not admit for a moment that Merrymarsh's imbecile prayer had any message for him. It was true that he had arranged with Mrs Rottingdean to return later that evening on the pretext that he had not finished reading the manuscript, excusing himself in the meantime by reference to the sherry party. But that had been an impulsive action, performed under the pressure of flustering circumstances. Now that he had escaped from that enchanted house of locked doors and inscrutable behaviour, he would not be fool enough to return. Or if, by any chance, he should return, he would contrive to lay his hands on the evidence of Merrymarsh's hidden life without embarking on a hidden life of his own with Virginia.

Yet, he had to acknowledge, it was a novel and not altogether disagreeable experience to have a nubile young woman throw herself at him with such wanton abandon. Before he had met Barbara, Adam's sexual experience had stopped short at holding the sticky hands of convent girls in the cinema, and perhaps coaxing from them afterwards a single tight-lipped kiss. The physical side of his long courtship of Barbara had been a tortured, intense affair of endless debate and limited action, an extended and nerve-racking exercise in erotic brinkmanship, marked by occasional skirmishes that were never, in the end, allowed to develop into major conflagrations. When they finally married they were clumsy, inexperienced lovers, and by the time they got the hang of it and began to enjoy themselves Barbara was six months pregnant. Ever since, pregnancy, actual or fearfully anticipated, had been a familiar attendant on their lovemaking. Adam had long resigned himself to this fate. The experience of unbridled sexuality, the casual, unpremeditated copulation un-embarrassed by emotional ties or practical consequences – the kind of thing that happened, he understood, between strangers at wild student parties, or to youthful electricians summoned to suburban villas on warm spring afternoons – this was not for him. He knew it only at second hand, passed to him in fragments of overheard conversation in bar or barrack room. *I tell you she had her belt and stockings off before I could close the door . . .! 'What's the matter?' she says. 'Nothing,' I says, 'I'm just looking for me screwdriver.' 'I bet you're good at screwing,' she says* . . . Now, it seemed, he had only to stretch out his hand to take such a plum for himself.

A precise tactile memory of Virginia's bare breast disturbed him with its sudden force, and he gripped the handlebars tightly. He tried to drive away temptation by thinking about Barbara; but she rose up in his imagination encumbered by children, a thermometer jutting from her mouth, a distracted frown wrinkling her brow.

You who made us pure as children . . .

He knew now why he couldn't get that wretched doggerel out of his mind: its rhythm exactly synchronized with the new knock that had developed in his engine.

The sherry party was in full swing by the time Adam arrived. Usually, on such occasions, the staff began drifting away just as the first ice began to melt; but tonight everyone seemed to have decided that in view of the fog it was pointless trying to get home in the rush-hour, so one might as well make a night of it. The single, fortunate, exception to this rule had been the bar-steward, who had departed leaving behind him a generous quantity of filled glasses. Adam, who had seldom felt so grievously in need of a drink, made a beeline for this inviting display.

The postgraduate sherry party was a regular feature of the first term of the academic year, designed to introduce students to staff and to each other. For many it was hail and farewell, since the Department did not have the resources to mount a proper graduate programme, and in any case espoused the traditional belief that research was a lonely and eremitic occupation, a test of character rather than learning, which might be vitiated by excessive human contact. As if they sensed this the new postgraduates, particularly those from overseas, roamed the floor eagerly accosting the senior guests, resolved to cram a whole year's sociability into one brief evening. As he left the bar with his first sherry, Adam was snapped up by a cruising Indian.

'Good evening. My name is Alibai.'

'Hallo. Mine's Appleby,' said Adam. Mr Alibai extended his hand and Adam shook it.

'How do you do,' said Mr Alibai.

'How do you do,' said Adam, who knew what was expected of him.

'You are a Professor at the University?'

'No, I'm a postgraduate.'

'I also. I am to write a thesis on Shani Hodder. You are acquainted with her work?'

'No, who is she?'

Mr Alibai looked dejected. 'I have not met a single person who has heard of Shani Hodder.'

'That happens to all of us,' said Adam. 'Have another sherry?'

'No thank you. I do not drink alcohol, and the fruit juices give the diarrhoea.'

'Well, excuse me. I'm terribly thirsty.' Adam pushed his way back to the bar. He drank two more dry sherries very quickly. His stomach, which was empty, made a noise like old plumbing. He looked around for food, but could only find a plate thinly covered with the crumbs of potato chips. These he ate greedily, picking them up on the moistened tips of his fingers. At the other side of the room he saw Camel, who waved. Adam gave him a cold stare and turned his back. He found himself face to face with a bald-headed man in a pale striped suit.

'What do you think of anus?' said the man.

'I beg your pardon?'

'The novelist, Kingsley Anus,' said the man impatiently.

'Oh, yes. I like his work. There are times when I think I belong to him more than to any of the others.'

'Please?' said the man, frowning.

'Well, you see, I have this theory,' Adam, who had just thought of it, said expansively. 'Has it ever occurred to you how novelists are *using up* experience at a dangerous rate? No, I see it hasn't. Well, then, consider that before the novel emerged as the dominant literary form, narrative literature dealt only with the extraordinary or the allegorical – with kings and queens, giants and dragons, sublime virtue and diabolic evil. There was no risk of confusing that sort of thing with life, of course. But as soon as the novel got going, you might pick up a book at any time and read about an ordinary chap called Joe Smith doing just the sort of things you did yourself. Now, I know what you're going to say – you're going to say that the novelist still has to invent a lot. But that's just the point: there've been such a fantastic number of novels written in the last couple of centuries that they've just about exhausted the possibilities of life. So all of us, you see, are really enacting events that have already been written about in some novel or other. Of course, most people don't realize this – they fondly imagine that their little lives are unique . . . Just as well, too, because when you *do* tumble to it, the effect is very disturbing.'

'Bravo!' said Camel, over Adam's shoulder. Adam ignored him, and eagerly searched the face of the bald-headed man for some response to his own remarks.

'Would you say,' said the man at length, 'that Anus is superior or inferior to C. P. Slow?'

'I don't know that you can compare them,' said Adam wearily.

'I have to: they are the only British novelists I have read.'

'Where have you been all the afternoon?' said Camel.

'I'm not talking to you,' said Adam, going to the bar and taking another sherry.

Camel followed him. 'What have I done?'

The dry sherry tasted like medicine. He put it down half-finished and tried a sweet one. 'You betrayed me to that man in the Museum.'

'What are you talking about?'

The sweet sherry tasted better, but he was conscious of two quite different sensations in his stomach. 'When that man was after me, you put him on my track. I *saw* you.'

It took a long time before Camel finally identified the man. 'Oh, *him!* He just had an application slip you'd filled in wrongly.'

Adam tried to look Camel straight in the eyes, but Camel's face kept bobbing about. 'Are you telling the truth?' he demanded.

'Of course I am. What did you think he wanted?'

'I thought he wanted to arrest me for raising the fire alarm.'

'Did you? Raise the fire alarm, I mean?' said Camel with wide eyes.

'Yes. No. I don't know.' He told Camel the whole story.

'I don't think you've anything to worry about,' said Camel in the end. 'No one's been asking questions about you. Except Barbara.'

'Barbara?'

'Yes, she came to the Museum, not long after you shot off.'

'I *thought* I saw her . . . What on earth did she want?'

'It seems they announced on the radio, a bit prematurely, that there was a fire in the Museum, and she wanted to find out if you were all right.'

'Poor Barbara. Was she terribly worried?'

'Well, not when she got there, of course. When she sent in a message for you I went out and took her and the kids for a cup of tea.'

Adam's tear-ducts pricked him. He gulped another sweet sherry. 'Camel, you're a good friend,' he whimpered. 'And Barbara is a good wife. I'm not worthy of either of you.'

'I'm afraid the confessor came out in me again,' said Camel, with a surprising and rather charming blush. 'Barbara told me she was afraid she was pregnant again.'

'What shall I do?' Adam appealed to him. 'How shall I house it? clothe it? feed it?'

'I was telling Barbara, I think you ought to throw yourself on the mercy of the Department – use this to twist their arm over the job situation.'

'D'you think it would do any good?'

'You have nothing to lose. Listen, do you know how Bane got his first promotion? He was telling me the other day: he'd been an assistant lecturer for six years without murmuring when one day his tank burst and he couldn't pay the plumber. He rushed straight into Howells' room and demanded promotion. Howells made him up on the spot and back-dated his pay six months. Seems it had just slipped his mind.'

'Good Lord,' said Adam.

'Incidentally, now Bane has got this new Chair, there should be a vacancy coming up.'

'There's the Prof in the corner,' said Adam, straightening his tie.

'I shouldn't go directly to him,' said Camel. 'Go through Briggs, who knows you better. He has the Prof's ear too.'

'I don't know that he has, any more,' said Adam, remembering the interview at lunch time. 'I think Bane is the coming man now.'

'Well, please yourself,' said Camel.

Adam felt a tug at his sleeve. It was the bald-headed man again.

'I told a lie,' he said. 'I have also read the work of John Bane.'

'Which John Bane?' said Adam carefully. 'The John Bane who wrote *Room at the Top*, or the John Bane who wrote *Hurry on Down*?'

'*The* John Bane,' said the man, frowning.

'Someone taking my name in vain?' boomed the Professor of Absurdist Drama, swooping down on them.

'In bane,' Adam quipped, and laughed immoderately.

The professor ignored him. 'Hallo, Camel,' he said. 'How's the research going?' Bane was Camel's current supervisor, the original one having died in office.

Camel took out his pipe, and began stuffing it with tobacco. 'I'm working on a new interpretation of *The Ambassadors*,' he said.

'Oh?' said Bane, tweaking the wings of his bow tie. He was in full fig this evening, wearing a corduroy jacket with wales so wide and deep that Adam imagined they must have a special purpose, like the indentations of snow-tyres.

'You remember how Strether refuses to tell Maria Gostrey the nature of the manufactured article on which the Newsome fortune is based?'

'I do indeed,' said Bane. Adam could not resist stroking the sleeve of his jacket, but the professor shook his hand off irritably.

'And you recall that James, quite typically, refuses to tell *us* what it is?' Camel went on. Bane nodded, and removed himself from Adam's reach. People near by pricked up their ears and began to drift towards Camel, who was always a draw. 'Strether describes it as a "small, trivial, rather ridiculous object of the commonest use", but "wanting in dignity". Scholars have argued for years about what it could be.' Camel paused to light his pipe, holding his audience in suspense. 'Well, I'm convinced that it was a chamber pot,' he said at last.

The girls among his listeners giggled and nudged each other. This was what they had come to hear.

'Once you see it, it becomes a symbol as important as the bowl in *The Golden Bowl*,' said Camel.

'Very interesting,' said Bane. 'And what do you think, Mr Appleby?'

'I think it was contraceptives,' said Adam.

There was a little shocked inspiration of breath among the girls. Bane flushed and stalked away. Camel took Adam to one side.

'I think you'd better stick to Briggs,' he said.

'What's wrong?' Adam complained. 'Isn't everyone entitled to his *idée fixe*? Anyway, you can't describe a chamber pot as small.'

'Bane thought you were getting at him,' said Camel. 'He was the one who stopped the College barber selling french letters.'

'Oh well,' said Adam. He took a medium sherry this time, hoping to effect some kind of reconciliation between the two sensations in his stomach.

'Hallo, Appleby.' It was Briggs. 'How are things with you?'

'Terrible,' Adam said. Camel beat a tactful retreat.

'Oh, I'm sorry to hear that. Blocked on the thesis?'

'Blocked on everything,' said Adam. 'Except paternity. My wife's going to have another baby.'

'Oh, congratulations. Your first?'

'No, our fourth.'

Briggs looked grave.

'I'm desperate,' Adam said. 'I can't get on with my work because I'm worrying all the time about my family. Our flat is full of beds already and I have nowhere to study. The children need new shoes and the electricity may be cut off at any moment. Yesterday the youngest child developed a rash: we think it's rickets.'

'Dear me,' said Briggs. 'This is very distressing.' He bit his lips and pulled on the lobes of his ears.

Adam raised his glass and drained it dramatically. 'This is my farewell to the academic life,' he said. 'Tomorrow I shall burn all my notes and take a job on the buses.'

'No, no, you mustn't be so impulsive,' said Briggs. 'I'll see what I can do.'

'What I need is a job,' said Adam firmly.

'I'll see what I can do,' Briggs repeated. 'Don't do anything rash.'

Adam watched him push his way through the throng towards Howells. As was his custom on such occasions, the Head of Department sat in a corner of the room with his back to the company, drinking with his constant companions, the two technicians who operated the professor's pride and joy, a computer for making concordances. Only senior members of staff generally ventured to approach this tiny court. Occasionally they would introduce some exceptionally promising postgraduate, but there were many students present who, when they eventually left the Department with their Ph.D.s, would only be able to say, with Moses, that they had seen the back parts of their Professor.

'I have decided to change the subject of my thesis,' said a voice at Adam's right ear. It was Mr Alibai.

'I'm sure you're wise,' said Adam. 'I couldn't see much future in Shani Hodder. Who was she, by the way?'

'She was an Anglo-Indian novelist. I should be most grateful if you would kindly suggest an alternative.'

'What about Egbert Merrymarsh?' said Adam. 'I could put you on to some interesting unpublished stuff of his.' Mr Alibai looked blank. 'He was a minor Catholic novelist and essayist,' Adam explained.

'I would prefer someone with Indian connections,' said Mr Alibai.

'Ah, there you have me,' Adam sighed.

'Or some unquestionably major figure. I thought the symbolism of D. H. Lawrence . . .'

'I have a feeling it's been done,' said Adam.

'Could I have a word with you, Appleby?'

Briggs was back again. He drew Adam aside, conspiratorially. 'There *will* be a vacancy coming up in the Department, as it happens,' he murmured. 'I've spoken to the Prof and he seemed quite favourably disposed.'

'That's wonderful,' said Adam. 'I didn't even know he knew who I was.'

'I put in a strong plea on the grounds of your . . . personal circumstances,' said Briggs. 'But there's no possibility of starting before next October.'

'Well, I can just about hang on till then,' said Adam. 'I can't thank you enough.'

'Don't go away,' said Briggs. 'I'll try to find an opportunity of getting him to speak to you.'

'Well?' said Camel, coming up as Briggs sloped off.

'It's unbelievable,' said Adam. 'Briggs seems to think that he's got me the job.'

'Good,' said Camel. 'I told you it was worth a try.'

Adam took another medium sherry by way of celebration. 'All shall be well and all manner of things shall be well,' he intoned happily. There was no need for him to return to the devious paths of Bayswater. He could forget the whole upsetting episode, settle down comfortably to work on his thesis again, and learn to be a kind and understanding husband. 'I'm going to phone Barbara,' he told Camel.

It took him a long time to get to the door. The sherry glass he held in his extended hand seemed, like a vain and overbearing dancing partner, to lead him through a series of involved looping movements, sudden changes of direction, rapid shuffles and dizzying spins. On all sides a babble of academic conversation dinned in his ears.

'My subject is the long poem in the nineteenth century . . .'

'Once you start looking for Freudian symbols . . .'

'This book on Browning . . .'

'Poe was quite right. It *is* a contradiction in terms . . .'

'. . . the diphthong in East Anglian dialects . . .'

'. . . everything's either round and hollow or long and pointed, when you come to think about it . . .'

'. . . is it called *The Bow and the Lyre* or *The Beau and the Liar* . . .?'

'So that's what *op. cit.* means!'

'. . . sort of *eeeow* . . .'

'. . . hasn't published a thing . . .'

'. . . "eighteenth-century gusto", and it came out "eighteenth-century gas-stove" . . .'

'No, like this: *eeeow* . . .'

'. . . waited three years for something to appear in *Notes and Queries* . . .'

'If it had been *"nineteenth*-century gas-stove" I might have got away with it . . .'

'. . . then the editors changed and they sent it back . . .'

'I thought it was short for "opposite" . . .'

'. . . *eeeow* . . .'

Three of the young men present were writing academic novels of manners. From time to time they detached themselves from the main group of guests and retired to a corner to jot down observations and witty remarks in little notebooks. Adam noticed one of them looking over the shoulders of the other two, and copying. He felt a tug at his sleeve.

'Mormon Nailer –' the bald-headed man began.

'Sorry,' said Adam. 'I have to make a phone call.'

A public phone was fixed to the wall of the corridor just outside the room in which the party was being held. Its little helmet of sound-proofing scarcely diminished the roar of conversation, and Adam held a finger in his left ear as he waited for Barbara to answer the phone. When she did so, her voice was unexpectedly sprightly.

'Hallo, darling,' she said. 'It's nice to hear your voice. I thought I was a widow this afternoon.'

'So I hear. I'm sorry I missed you.'

'Never mind, Camel was sweet and gave us tea. Where were you all the afternoon, anyway?'

'Oh, er, I was out . . . researching. Listen, I have good news.'

'What kind of research?'

'It's a long story. I'll tell you later. How are you feeling?'

'I'm feeling much better.'

'Better?' he echoed her uneasily.

'Yes, I went over the charts again and I convinced myself we made a mistake. I felt better immediately. Adam, I'm sure I'm not pregnant.'

'Nonsense!' he shouted. 'Of course you're pregnant!' A couple who were leaving the party gave him odd looks as they passed.

'What do you mean, Adam?'

'I mean, you're so long overdue, and felt sick this morning,' he continued, in more controlled tones. 'Sure signs.'

'But I ate my breakfast in the end.'

'Yes, but only marmalade. I distinctly remember it was only marmalade. It was a craving.'

'Adam, you sound as if you *wanted* me to be pregnant.'

'I do, I do,' he moaned. 'I've just talked Briggs into getting me a job in the Department. But he's only doing it because he thinks we're going to have another baby!'

'Oh,' said Barbara.

'That was my good news,' he said bitterly.

Barbara was silent for a few moments. Then she said, 'Well, look, if it's absolutely essential for us to have another baby to get this job, we can easily arrange it.'

He considered the idea for a few moments, and found it repellent. 'No,' he said. 'Falling for another baby and getting a job in consequence is a pleasant surprise. But having to conceive another baby to get a job is quite another matter. No job is worth it.'

'I agree,' said Barbara. 'But what will you do?'

'I'll just have to bluff it out,' said Adam. 'I can always say you had a miscarriage, I suppose.'

When Adam returned to the party he found Camel talking to Pond.

'Hallo, what are you doing here?' he said.

'Camel invited me to drop in,' said Pond. 'Lot of wogs you have here.'

Adam looked round nervously for Mr Alibai and located him

on the other side of the room. The Indian interpreted his look as a summons, and came over.

'You have a subject for me?' he said eagerly.

'No, but I want you to meet Mr Pond,' said Adam. 'He is a great expert on Anglo-Indian relations.'

'I am most honoured,' said Mr Alibai, extending his hand to Pond. 'How do you do?'

Adam drew Camel aside. 'Look, it seems Barbara may not be pregnant after all.'

'Congratulations,' said Camel.

'Yes, but what shall I do about this job?'

'Say nothing, old chap. If you have to show up with four children on occasion, you can always borrow one.'

'Ah, there you are, Appleby,' said Briggs. 'The Prof would like to have a word with you.'

Camel gave Adam an encouraging pat on the shoulder, which Briggs observed suspiciously. 'I hope you haven't been talking about this matter to anyone, Appleby,' he said, as he steered Adam across the floor. 'There are all kinds of forces at play in the academic world, as you will discover for yourself. Discretion is vital. Mum's the word.'

Adam fought back an urge to confess that mum wasn't the word. He stood behind Howells' broad back, dry-mouthed and trembling, as Briggs stooped to whisper in the professor's ear. Howells turned his big, bloodshot eyes upon Adam.

'It's Appleby I wanted to see,' he said to Briggs.

'This *is* Mr Appleby, Prof.'

'No, Briggs. This is Camel.'

'I assure you –'

'It's Appleby I want, Briggs. The one who's working on sewage in the nineteenth century or some such thing. Bright man – Bane told me about him. You've got them mixed up.' He gave a short, barking laugh, and turned back to his cronies.

'Tell Appleby I want to see him,' he threw over his shoulder.

'I'll tell him,' said Adam, speaking for the first time.

'I'm sorry,' said Briggs, as they walked away. 'There seems to have been a misunderstanding.'

'Forget it,' said Adam.

Briggs bit his lip and pulled violently on the lobes of his ears. 'Someone I could mention has been intriguing behind my back,' he muttered.

Adam went over to Camel. 'Well?' said Camel.

'Congratulations,' said Adam.

Camel raised his eyebrows.

'Howells wants to see you.'

'Me?'

'Your name is Appleby, isn't it?'

'What are you talking about?'

'You're writing a thesis on sanitation in Victorian fiction?'

'You know I am . . .'

'Well, you've got a job. Howells is waiting to bestow it on you.'

Camel lolloped across the room, pausing occasionally to cast a quizzical, distrustful glance at Adam. Adam waved him on impatiently. He turned back to the bar, where Pond was discoursing to Mr Alibai with every sign of friendly animation.

'Well, we've sorted out Mr Alibai's little problem,' Pond said. 'He's going to work on the influence of the *Kama Sutra* on contemporary fiction.'

'I envy you,' said Adam to Mr Alibai, who gave a proud, shy smile.

'I am most indebted . . .' he murmured.

'Nice chap,' said Pond, when final handshakes had been exchanged. 'He's going to enrol in my Advanced English Course.'

'But he doesn't need it.'

'No, he doesn't, but he seems struck on me. It's a fatal gift I have. By the way, Adam, I was pulling your leg about my limp at lunch time.'

'Oh?'

'Yes, you see Sally and I sometimes take a shower together, and –'

'Telephone for you, Adam,' said someone.

'Hallo? Is that you, Adam?'

'Don't tell me, let me guess,' said Adam. 'You feel pregnant again.'

'How did you know?'

'It had to be that. The job has fallen through.'

'Oh, *darling*! And I thought you'd be pleased. Why?'

The party was breaking up at last, and the corridor was full of noisy people putting on hats and coats. Adam turned a stony gaze upon them, holding his finger to his ear in the attitude of a man about to commit suicide.

'Can't tell you now. Later.'

'How much later, Adam? Are you coming home now?'

'I have to go to the Museum to pick up my things.'

'But it's closed by now.'

'No, it's open late tonight.'

'Well, you're not going to stay there, are you?'

'Yes,' he said on a sudden impulse. 'Yes, I think I'll stay and do some work. Don't wait up for me.'

He put down the receiver quickly, before Barbara could bring any pathos or moral suasion to bear on him. He had reached the moment of decision, and he did not wish to be swayed from his purpose. He would return to Bayswater. He would get his hands on Merrymarsh's scandalous confessions, and with them he would deal a swingeing blow at the literary establishment, at academe, at Catholicism, at fate. He would publish his findings to the world, and leap to fame or perdition in a blaze of notoriety.

As he walked unsteadily away from the phone, the people in the corridor falling back before him, he thought of himself as a man set apart by a dangerous quest. For what was that house in

Bayswater, dismal of aspect and shrouded in fog, with its mad, key-rattling old queen, raven-haired, honey-tongued daughter, and murderous minions insecurely pent in the dungeon below, but a Castle Perilous from which, mounted on his trusty scooter, he, intrepid Sir Adam, sought to snatch the unholy grail of Egbert Merrymarsh's scrofulous novel? If the success of this quest, contrary to the old story, necessitated his fall from grace in the arms of the seductive maiden, then so much the better. He had had enough of continence.

Adam swaggered through the doorway intent on a final sherry. He had omitted, however, to remove his finger from his ear. His projecting elbow struck the door jamb, and this trivial collision was enough, it seemed, to level him to the floor. Several departing guests trod on him before Camel and Pond came to the rescue.

9

'Human Fertility', formerly the 'Journal of Contraception'.

Item in the British Museum Catalogue

There was only one shop open in the section of the Edgware Road where Adam had parked his scooter. The window was brightly lit, but it was invisible from a distance of twelve paces on either side. Adam was quite sure of this figure because he had walked past the shop about twenty-five times so far.

He had sobered up considerably since leaving the sherry party. Camel and Pond had carried him to the Gents and put his head under a cold tap. Then they had taken him to a coffee bar and made him consume a cheese sandwich and three cups of bitter black espresso. Their efforts had been kindly meant, but he rather wished they hadn't done their work so thoroughly; in the process he had mislaid that happy mood of careless confidence in which his resolution to return to Bayswater had been formed. He struggled in vain to recover the image of himself as a swash-buckling adventurer, bent single-mindedly on his purpose, but prepared to accept imperturbably whatever willing female flesh chance threw in his path. All day circumstances had cracked the whip and urged him through a bewildering variety of hoops, but so far he had not been at a loss for a style in which to negotiate them. Now, when he most needed to assume a ready-made role, the knack seemed to have deserted him. He was alone with himself again, the old Adam, a bare forked animal with his own peculiar moral problem.

There were, of course, plenty of unfaithful husbands in literature: modern fiction, in particular, might be described as a compendium of advice on the conduct of adultery. But he couldn't, off-hand, recall one who, distracted and frustrated by the complexities of the married relation, had sought relief in the willing arms of another woman only to find himself trammelled by the very same absurd scruples from which he had fled.

He paused yet again in front of the shop window. The defective neon sign above it flickered dimly in the fog: URGICALGODS. He had need of the urgical gods – he longed to be possessed by the spirit of Dionysian abandon; but this shrine did not throw him into a transport of profane joy. On the contrary, he eyed the contents of the window with feelings of disquiet and repugnance. *Sexual Happiness Without Fear* was the title of one of the books for sale. But it was not only the two flanking volumes, *The History of Flagellation* and *Varieties of Venereal Disease*, which gave the cheerfulness of the first title a forced and hollow note. It was also the trusses, elastic stockings and male corsets, displayed on pink plastic limbs that were oddly like the gruesome votive objects, signifying cures, that hung in the side-chapels of Spanish churches. Still more it was the abundance of little boxes, jars and packets, these guaranteeing a spectacular development of the bust, those offering new hope to the older man, others more enigmatically labelled, containing, as he knew, the instruments of carefree pleasure, but bearing trade names suggestive of medicaments. The whole display was decidedly detumescent in effect, projecting a vision of sexuality as a universal illness, its sufferers crippled hypochondriacs, trussed and bandaged, anointed with hormone cream, hipped on rejuvenation pills, who owed their precarious survival entirely to artificial aids and appliances.

He turned away and recommenced his pacing of the pavement. There was no doubt, he thought wryly, that the conditioning of a Catholic upbringing and education entered into the very marrow of a man. It unfitted him for the prosecution of an *affaire* with the proper gaiety and confidence. The taking of 'precautions' which was, no doubt, to the secular philanderer a process as mechanical and thoughtless as blinking, was to him an ordeal imbued with embarrassment, guilt and superstitious fear; and one which, Adam now saw, might easily come to overshadow in moral importance the act of sexual licence itself.

Perhaps, he tried to persuade himself, his anxiety was misplaced. Virginia was surely the kind of girl who felt underdressed if she wasn't wearing a diaphragm. Couldn't he safely leave that side of things to her? But something told him she was not as experienced as she pretended – how could she be, with that old dragon, her mother, breathing down her neck? Besides, after Barbara's proved incompetence to operate the Safe Method successfully, he no longer trusted women in the conduct of such matters. One slip on Virginia's part and nine months from now he might be the unwilling father of not merely one but two new offspring.

The possibility smote him with such appalling force that he all but abandoned the enterprise there and then. But somehow he couldn't contemplate going home with nothing to cheer him in the face of looming domestic problems. The events of the day lay about him like ruins. Though he had selfishly occupied a seat in the Reading Room since the morning, he hadn't opened a single book; furthermore, he had thrown the British Museum into panic and disorganization, falsely suspected a friend of treachery, lost a job after enjoying it for ten minutes and disgraced himself in the eyes of the Department. Overshadowing and darkening all these setbacks were the prognostications of another addition to the Appleby family. If he could return home with Merrymarsh's secret manuscript, that at least would be something achieved, something to go to bed on, dreaming of a brighter future.

It wasn't, in other words, simple lust that had driven him thus far towards the house in Bayswater; it was the lure of a literary discovery. Virginia was just a contingency – though not entirely regretted, he had to admit. In fact, to be quite honest, he looked upon her in the light of a bonus: if the question of Merrymarsh's manuscript hadn't arisen, he wouldn't for a moment have entertained the idea of jumping into bed with her; but if jumping into bed was the only way of getting his hands on the manuscript . . . well, he was only human. Either way, of course, it was what Father Bonaventure would have called a grave sin; but he was in no mood to let that deter him – indeed he looked forward to the experience of being a Sinner in full-blooded style with a certain grim satisfaction. The advantage of the present circumstances was that they permitted him to feel the victim of an almost irresistible temptation which was not of his seeking. And a small voice inside him hinted that if he was going to be unfaithful to Barbara, if he was going to have one wild fling at forbidden fruit, then he could scarcely do so with greater ease, secrecy and freedom from remorse than now.

The very elements seemed to have conspired to draw a discreet veil round his moment of decision. The Edgware Road was eerily silent and deserted. Occasionally the hush was dissipated by a bus, crawling by in low gear, its windows becoming palely visible as it drew level, only to fade again almost immediately. At long intervals a pedestrian, coughing and muffled in scarves, stumbled past and was swallowed up in the anonymity of the fog. If he could not find the courage now to embark on an amorous adventure, what chance was there of his ever doing so in more normal meteorological conditions? It was now or never. Adam braced himself and stepped purposefully towards the shop.

As he did so he heard the sound of footsteps on the pavement behind him. He was tempted to stop and skulk against a wall while the pedestrian passed on, but knew that if he hesitated again he would never recover his resolution. He accelerated his pace, but the footsteps followed suit. He broke into a trot, and heard his pursuer coughing and panting as he strove to overtake. The brightly-lit glass door of the shop loomed up suddenly, and Adam reached for the latch. As he did so, a heavy hand caught him by the shoulder, and he froze in the attitude of an arrested thief.

'Excuse me, sir,' said an Irish voice, 'but am I anywhere at all near the Marble Arch?'

'Keep going, and you'll come to it,' Adam replied. He averted his head from his questioner as he spoke, but his attempt to disguise his voice was unsuccessful.

'Glory be to God, is it yourself, Mr Appleby?' said Father Finbar.

'Were you going in here, Mr Appleby? Don't let me stop you.'

'Oh, it's all right, Father –'

'I'll come in with you. I wouldn't mind getting out of this fog myself, for a minute or two.'

'Let me show you where Marble Arch –'

'Tell me inside, Mr Appleby. Mother of God, did you ever see the likes of this weather?'

Father Finbar took Adam firmly by the arm and led him, struggling feebly, into the shop. A small, dapper man with a toothbrush moustache was sitting on a stool behind the counter, reading a newspaper. He got to his feet with a discreet smile of welcome. As Father Finbar unwound his scarf and revealed his dog-collar, the man's smile slowly hardened into an unnatural grin, a rictus of shock behind which feelings of incredulity, curiosity and fear seemed to be struggling for ascendancy. Father Finbar rattled on comfortably.

'Did I never tell you, Mr Appleby, I have a cousin who's at the Oratory up at Brompton there and being up in Town today, and having the afternoon to myself which doesn't happen very often I thought I'd take the opportunity of dropping in on him. But it was a bad move and no mistake. I've been waiting since five for the fog to clear and I'm blessed if I don't think it's worse now than it was then. So I decided to hoof it in the end. Shocking weather, mister,' he concluded, addressing the man behind the counter, who responded by nodding his head several times, his countenance still distorted by the vacant grin. 'I suppose you think I shouldn't be complaining about fog with the brogue on me, but Irish mist is a different proposition entirely. You could stand a broomstick up in this stuff and it wouldn't fall down. Bad for business too, I suppose?'

'Can I do anything for you gentlemen?' said the man.

Father Finbar looked expectantly at Adam, who raked the shelves desperately for some innocuous purchase. His eyes lighted thankfully on a carton of paper tissues.

'Kleenex, please. The small packet.'

'Sixpence,' said the man.

'Aye, the fog gets right up your nose, doesn't it. Filthy stuff, I'm half choked m'self,' said Father Finbar. 'Could I have a packet of throat lozenges?' he said.

'We don't stock them,' said the man.

'Don't stock them?' Father Finbar repeated, looking round him in surprise. 'This is a chemist's shop, isn't it?'

'No –' the man began.

'It's only a step to the Marble Arch, Father,' said Adam, cutting in swiftly and loudly. 'Then you can walk down Park Lane to Hyde Park Corner and along Grosvenor Place and that brings you to Victoria, and if I were you –'

'Aye, I'll be on my way in a moment,' said Father Finbar. 'You know Adam – you don't mind if I call you Adam? – you know I'm very glad we bumped into each other, because I've been thinking about that most interesting conversation we had this morning.'

'Oh, it's not worth talking about,' said Adam deprecatingly, edging towards the door.

'Oh, but it is. It was most in-ter-est-ing. I'm thinking you feel the Church is too hard on young married folk –'

'Oh no, no, not at all!' Adam protested. He opened the door, but Father Finbar showed no inclination to budge.

'Don't leave the door open, please,' said the man behind the counter. 'It lets the fog in.'

'That's right, just hold your horses, Adam,' said Father Finbar. He turned to the man. 'You don't mind us taking a breather here for a moment, do you, mister? An empty shop is bad for trade, isn't that right?'

'It's the other way round in my line of business,' said the man, who seemed to be recovering his self-possession. He looked suspiciously at Adam and Father Finbar as if he suspected he was the victim of a hoax.

'Is that so?' said Father Finbar curiously. 'Now, why would that be the case?'

'What were you saying about our conversation this morning, Father?' said Adam, leaping desperately from the frying pan to the fire.

'Ah, yes, now where was I? I was meaning to say, Adam, that you mustn't think the Church forbids birth control just to make life harder for young couples.'

'Of course not –'

'It's just a matter of teaching God's law. It's a simple question of right and wrong . . .' His voice, which had been so far mild and gentle, suddenly rose to the pitch of a pulpit-thumping tirade. 'CONTRACEPTION IS NOTHING LESS THAN THE MURDER OF GOD-GIVEN LIFE AND THE PEOPLE WHO MAKE AND SELL THE FILTHY THINGS ARE AS GUILTY AS THOSE WHO SUPPLY OPIUM TO DRUG ADDICTS!' he roared.

'Here,' said the man behind the counter. 'You can't say things like that to me.'

'This is a private religious discussion,' Father Finbar retorted with a fierce look, 'and I'll thank you to keep your opinions to yourself.' He turned back to Adam. 'Did you know,' he went on in a vibrant whisper, 'that the manufacture of contraceptives is an industry so vast that no one can even make a guess at the profits? that the whole dirty trade is so covered up with shame and secrecy that these profiteers don't even pay taxes? that the whole affair is actively encouraged and supported by the Communists to sap the vitality of the West.'

'No,' said Adam, keeping his eye on the man behind the counter. He was surreptitiously using the telephone, and Adam had no doubt that he was calling the police. 'Don't you think we'd better be going, Father?' he pleaded.

'Perhaps so,' said the priest, raising his voice. 'Some people in this world don't like to hear unpleasant truths.' When they were outside on the pavement he said to Adam: 'You know, I shouldn't be surprised if our man back there didn't deal in the things himself.'

'No!' said Adam.

'Oh, yes. I shouldn't be surprised at all. Under the counter, you know, under the counter . . . And what are you doing here, Adam?'

'I was just buying some paper handkerchiefs,' said Adam, eagerly brandishing the evidence under the priest's nose. He broke open the packet and blew his nose vigorously.

'No, I mean what are you doing in the Edgware Road? Lost your way?'

'Oh. No, I was on my way to . . . some friends. In Bayswater.'

'They must be very good friends to keep you out on a night like this. I'm off home myself. It's going to be a long walk, but I have my rosary in my pocket so the time won't be wasted. Is this the way to the Marble Arch? Good night then, and God bless you.'

'Good night, Father.'

Adam watched the priest melt into the fog. For some reason his broad-brimmed trilby was the last feature to disappear from sight, and for a second or two Adam had the impression that a disembodied hat was sailing gently down the Edgware Road. Then the hat was gone. Adam tiptoed to his scooter and pushed it softly in the opposite direction.

Adam knocked on the front door, but it was the hairy man who opened it. 'Come in,' he said. In his mutilated left hand he held a long knife.

'I'll come back later,' said Adam.

'No. Mrs said you must come in.'

Adam glanced over the man's shoulder and saw Virginia on the stairs. She nodded vigorously and beckoned. Adam stepped hesitantly over the threshold. 'Where is Mrs Rottingdean?' he asked.

'Out,' said the man. 'She has to collect a wreath.'

'Who for?' said Adam, eyeing the knife.

The hairy man was distracted by Virginia. 'Get back to your room, you,' he said. Virginia pouted and retreated up the stairs, swinging her hips. 'Bad lot,' the man commented. He threw open the door of the sitting-room. The manuscript of *Lay Sermons and Private Prayers* was on the chair where Adam had left it. 'You read – I watch,' said the hairy man. He sat down on the sofa and took out of his pocket a piece of emery paper with which he began to sharpen his knife.

'Where are you from?' said Adam conversationally.

'Argentina. Mrs said I must not talk. You read – I watch.'

Adam opened the manuscript at random and stared at it unseeingly for a few minutes. 'I don't like reading with someone watching me,' he said at length. 'Could you wait outside?'

'No,' said the hairy man, testing the blade of his knife on his thumb.

The door opened and Virginia came in.

'I said, get back to your room,' growled the hairy man. 'Your ma said you stays in your room till she gets back.'

'All right, Edmundo,' said Virginia demurely. 'I just thought I'd tell you there's an Elizabeth Taylor film on the television.'

The hairy man stiffened and regarded Virginia suspiciously. 'I'm not watching telly tonight,' he muttered. 'I'm watching him.'

'All right. I just thought I'd tell you,' said Virginia, making to go out.

'What movie is it, then?' said the hairy man.

'*National Velvet*,' said Virginia. 'Her first big picture – when she was just a girl. Fresh as a flower. Sweet, innocent. You'd love it, Edmundo.'

'I haven't seen it,' said the hairy man, licking his lips.

'You could leave the doors open,' said Virginia. 'Mr Appleby will be quite safe.'

The hairy man was silent for a moment. 'You turn the telly on and go back to your room,' he said at length. 'And I'll see.'

Virginia went out, leaving the door open. After a minute or two the sounds of hoof-beats and girlish cries were wafted faintly to their ears. Virginia passed in the hall and winked at Adam. They heard her go up the stairs, and her door slammed.

Two minutes passed: Adam counted them by the mournful tick of the grandfather clock in the hall. Then the hairy man got to his feet. 'You stay here, right? You want anything, you knock on the wall.' He demonstrated with the knuckle of his good hand.

'All right,' Adam said.

The hairy man thrust the knife into his belt and left the room.

The clock was striking the quarter hour when Virginia came downstairs again. She poked her head into the sitting-room, her eyes bright.

'Come on,' she whispered.

Adam gripped the arms of his chair. 'What about that man?' he hissed.

Virginia beckoned by way of reply. He followed her on

tiptoe to the open door of the adjoining room. 'Look,' she said.

Adam peeped in. The hairy man was sound asleep in front of the television set. His mouth was open and he snored gently.

'It never fails,' said Virginia.

'What about the other two men?' whispered Adam, as they crept upstairs.

'They're locked in the basement. Don't worry about them.'

'Who are they?'

'I told you – butchers.'

'He said he was from Argentina.'

'My father had a meat business there – he brought them over. God knows why – they're very careless at their job.'

'You mean . . . the fingers?'

Virginia nodded. 'Mother runs the business now, though she tries to pretend she doesn't. Well, here's my little love nest.'

She opened the door of a bedroom and switched on the light. Panting slightly from the long climb, Adam went in.

The room was a teenage slum. The bed, dressing-table and bookshelves evidently provided insufficient surface space for Virginia's possessions, most of which were strewn over the floor: books, magazines, records, dolls, sweaters, trousers, combs, brushes, cushions, scissors, nail-files, and jars – jars of cold cream, jars of nail polish, jars of bath salts, jars of sweets, even jars of jam. Discarded stockings and underwear had drifted up against one corner of the room. Pinned to the walls were seaside postcards, travel posters, a life-size portrait of the Beatles and a photograph of Virginia in her First Communion dress. It all made her seem much younger than she looked.

Virginia switched on the bedside lamp and turned off the main light. She locked the door and put her arms round Adam's waist. 'Isn't this fun?' she murmured, nestling up to him.

Adam was still holding the manuscript of *Lay Sermons and Private Prayers*, and he clasped it to his chest as a buffer between himself and Virginia. 'The papers,' he said.

Virginia pouted and disengaged herself. 'I'm not going to let you read them here,' she said. 'You can take them away. Time's too precious.'

'You promised to let me see them,' he said.

'Just a peep then.' She went to a cupboard and took out a hat-box, which she presented to Adam with a curtsy. He opened it, and took out a sheaf of letters rolled up in an elastic band and a thick exercise book. Both letters and book were charred at the edges, and a few flakes of burned paper fell back into the box as he lifted the documents out. He removed the elastic band with great care.

'I can't see properly,' he complained. 'Turn the light on again.'

'Sit on the bed,' said Virginia.

He went over to the bed and sat down near the lamp. Virginia joined him and began taking off her stockings. But he was soon lost in his discovery.

And it was a discovery. The letters were important only as verifying Virginia's story about Merrymarsh and her mother. Some of them were love letters, written in a mawkish sentimental style with a lot of baby-talk; others were brief notes, assignations, cancellations. But the book – the book was quite another matter. Adam riffled the pages with gathering excitement.

Entitled *Robert and Rachel* (pseudonyms for Merrymarsh and Mrs Rottingdean) it told, in the form of Robert's journal, the story of a middle-aged man's first love affair. Robert was a bachelor, a man of letters with a modest reputation, a popular apologist for Catholicism. At the age of forty-eight he had nothing to look forward to but a repetition of his existing routine, a gentle decline into the tranquillity of old age, a pious death, respectful obituaries in the Catholic press. Then, by a train of circumstances which seemed improbable though evidently based on fact, he was left alone in his country cottage for several days with a young girl, the niece of his housekeeper. One day he blundered into a room where she was bathing herself. He had

148

never seen a grown woman naked in his life before, and the sight unleashed in him an overpowering desire of which he had never dreamt he was capable. After prolonged and feverish skirmishing, hampered by inexperience and guilt on both sides, they became lovers. Then the housekeeper returned, the niece had to return to London. He begged her to marry him, but she refused, saying they would never be able to respect each other after what had passed. He followed her back to London, and they resumed the relationship, now as mistress and keeper . . .

At this point the story broke off. There had evidently been another exercise book which had been burned. It was a great pity. *Robert and Rachel* wasn't quite a literary work of art: it was feeling crude and unrefined, turned out clumsily from the rough moulds of real experience. There was a kind of embarrassment, a shamefulness in the confessions, from which no detail was spared, of a man whose sexual desire was ignited for the first time at the very moment when his sexual vigour was declining. It wasn't really art, and of course it hadn't been intended for publication; but it was unquestionably the best thing Egbert Merrymarsh had ever done. That description of the young girl, for instance, standing nude in the tin tub, her hair falling to her waist . . . As Adam turned back to read the passage again, the manuscript was snatched from his hands.

'That's quite enough,' said Virginia.

Adam's protest died in his throat. Virginia was sitting beside him, quite naked.

'You don't really want to go through with this, Virginia?' Adam pleaded, pacing up and down the room.

'You promised.'

'No, I didn't really promise . . . Anyway, your mother may come back at any moment. And that man –'

'She's gone to a wreath maker in Swiss Cottage and she'll be gone hours in this fog.'

'What does she want a wreath for, anyway?'

'For Merrymarsh. I think she has a little wreath-laying ceremony in store for you.'

'Good Lord! Where is he buried?'

'You're deliberately wasting time, Adam,' she accused him. 'I've kept my side of the bargain. Now it's your turn.'

'But why? Why? Why pick on me? I'm not the kind of man you're looking for. I'm no good in bed. I don't have enough practice.'

'You look kind. And gentle.'

Adam looked at her with suspicion.

'Have you . . . that is . . . are you a virgin?'

She flushed. 'Of course not.'

'How old are you?'

'Nineteen.'

'That's a lie.'

'Seventeen.'

'How do I know whether to believe you? You might be a minor for all I know.'

Virginia climbed on to the bed and took down her First Communion picture. She pointed to the record of her age and the date at the bottom.

'All right, so you're seventeen,' Adam said. 'Doesn't that picture make you feel any shame?'

'No,' said Virginia.

'Well, for God's sake put some clothes on,' said Adam. 'You make me feel cold.'

Virginia's response was to light the gas fire. 'Is that all I make you feel?' she said, a little sadly, as she crouched over the fire.

'No,' Adam admitted, watching the reflected glow of the gas fire deepen on her skin.

She came towards him radiantly. 'Take me, Adam,' she whispered. She took his hand and placed it over her breast. Adam groaned and closed his eyes.

'I can't, Virginia. I daren't. I haven't . . . taken precautions.'

'Don't worry about that, darling,' she murmured in his ear. Her breath made his skin tingle. With his free hand he began to stroke her back.

'You mean . . .' he said hoarsely, letting his fingers slide down her spine.

'I don't mind taking a chance.'

He opened his eyes and jumped back. *'Are you mad?'*

She came after him. 'I don't, really I don't.'

'Well, I do,' Adam said. He sat down, feeling faint. He had nearly lost control that time. He racked his brains for some further means of procrastination. 'Have you got a thermometer,' he said.

'Yes, I think so. Why?'

'If you really want to go through with this, you'll have to take your temperature.'

'You are a funny man.' With an air of humouring him, Virginia rummaged in the drawer of her dressing-table and withdrew, from a jumble of broken combs, broken jewellery, broken fountain-pens and broken rosaries, a miraculously un-broken thermometer. He took it from her and, having shaken down the mercury, slid it under her tongue.

'Sit on the bed,' he ordered.

She looked like a naughty child, sitting there naked with the thermometer in her mouth. Adam drew up a chair and took a paper and pencil from his pocket.

'Now, how long was the shortest of your last three periods?' he inquired.

Virginia spat out the thermometer. 'I haven't the foggiest,' she said. 'What is this all about?'

Adam replaced the thermometer. 'I'm trying to determine whether this is a safe time for relations,' he explained.

'Not very romantic,' Virginia seemed indistinctly to say.

'Sex isn't,' he snapped back. He plucked the thermometer

out and examined it. '97.6,' he announced, and wrote the figure down. He stood up and began to collect the Merrymarsh papers with the air of a doctor at the end of a consultation. 'Now, if you'll just go on taking your temperature every night and drop me a line when it rises sharply for three consecutive days, we'll see what we can do.' He gave her a bland smile.

Virginia jumped off the bed.

'You beast, you're just teasing me.'

'No, no, really.' He backed away.

'Yes you are. I've lost my patience, Adam.'

'Honestly, Virginia, it would be the height of folly –'

He reversed round the room, with Virginia in hot pursuit. Stockings entangled themselves round his ankles, and jars rolled under his feet. The back of his knees struck the edge of the bed, and he toppled back on to the counterpane. Virginia gave a little shriek of glee and threw herself upon him. He felt her fingers undoing his belt, and his trousers slowly receding. He struggled to retain them, but, on a sudden inspiration, desisted.

'Oh,' said Virginia. She got up and stepped back. 'Oh,' she said again. She snatched up a dressing-gown and held it in front of her. 'What are you wearing those for?'

Adam stood up, and his trousers fell to his feet. He fingered the lace on Barbara's pants. 'I've been trying to tell you all the evening,' he said in a broken voice. 'I'm . . . funny that way. I told you I wasn't the kind of man you're looking for.'

Virginia put on the dressing-gown and knotted the cord. 'You mean, you're really a woman?' she said, with wide eyes.

'No, no! I've got three children, remember.'

'Then why . . .?'

'Religion has played havoc with my married life,' he explained. 'If sex can't find its normal outlets . . .' He shrugged, and snapped the elastic on Barbara's pants.

The silence that followed this confession was broken by a

sudden uproar from downstairs. 'Mother!' said Virginia. She opened the door and hung over the bannister. Holding his trousers up with both hands, Adam followed her.

At the bottom of the stair-well, Mrs Rottingdean could be seen haranguing the hairy man, who was rubbing his eyes stupidly and trying to evade the blows aimed at his head. Mrs Rottingdean was carrying an immense wreath of holly and yew, which she finally pulled over the man's head. She unlocked the door leading to the basement, and the other two men tumbled out, wielding meat-axes. With dramatic gestures Mrs Rottingdean urged them up the stairs.

Adam fled back to the bedroom. Virginia followed and locked the door.

'What shall I do?' said Adam frantically.

'There's a fire escape,' said Virginia, throwing up the sash of her window. 'I'll say you went hours ago, while Edmundo was asleep.'

'And the papers?'

'You can keep them,' said Virginia dejectedly. 'I don't suppose I'll have another chance to use them.'

Adam scooped up the papers and stepped to the window. 'I'm sorry, Virginia,' he said, and implanted a chaste kiss on her forehead.

Virginia sniffed. 'And I did so want to be the first sixth-former in St Monica's to do it,' she said.

'So you are a virgin after all?'

She nodded, and two tears trickled down her cheeks.

'Never mind,' said Adam consolingly. 'There'll be other opportunities.'

Mrs Rottingdean's myrmidons pounded up the last flight of stairs. 'You'd better go,' said Virginia.

As Adam stepped on to the fire escape, his trousers slipped down again. To save time, he took them off and wound them round the Merrymarsh papers. The fog coiled damply round his bare legs, but he was grateful for its cover. As he cautiously descended the ladder he was conscious of re-enacting one of the oldest roles in literature.

IO

Now I find the evenings intolerable after the
British Museum closes; and think you might let me have
something to read by way of change.

Baron Corvo (Letter to Grant Richards)

Adam crawled wearily into the Reading Room just as the bell stridently announced that the Library would close in fifteen minutes. As he sank on to his padded seat everyone around him began standing up, pushing back their chairs, yawning, stretching, sorting their papers and arranging their books. Many of them had been there all day: their countenances were fatigued but contented, conveying the satisfaction of work well done – so many books read, so many notes taken. Then there were the Night People of the Museum – those writing books or theses while holding down day-time jobs. Hurrying from their offices to the Museum through the rush-hour, pausing only to snatch a quick meal at Lyons, they worked through the evening with fierce and greedy concentration. Now they looked reproachfully at the clock, and continued reading even as they stood in line to return their books. Adam felt an imposter in this company, especially when they stood respectfully aside as he carried his huge, tottering pile of unread Lawrentiana to the central counter.

'I want to reserve them all,' he said, and returned to his desk to collect his belongings. A man tapped him on the shoulder and waved an application slip.

'Mr Appleby, isn't it? I think you've got the press-mark wrong on this one.'

'Oh, yes,' said Adam, taking the slip. 'Thank you. I'll see to it tomorrow.'

The desk next to his was vacant. Camel had gone home. But he had left a note for Adam.

> The job I have been offered is a fiendish plot to make me finish my thesis. Bane just told me I shall be on probation until I get my Ph.D. Doubtless I shall be the first university teacher to retire while still on probation. – C.

Adam smiled, and lifted his duffle coat from the back of the seat. Another note fell out of the hood.

> A new proposal for the statute book – *Academic Publications Act:* 'The Government will undertake to subsidize the publication of a monthly periodical, about the size of a telephone directory and printed in columns on Bible paper, which will publish all scholarly articles, notes, correspondence etc. submitted to it, irrespective of merit or interest. All existing journals will be abolished. This will eliminate the element of invidious competition in academic appointments and promotions, which will be offered to candidates in alphabetical order.' (With your initials you shouldn't have any trouble.) – C.

Adam grinned and shrugged on his duffle coat. He felt in his pockets for his gloves, and pulled out two more missives. One was a clipping of the Brownlong ad., with a message scrawled across it: 'Why don't you go in for this? – C.' The other read:

> What about:
>
> > I always choose a Brownlong chair,
> > Professors use them everywhere.

Or:

> I always choose a Brownlong chair:
> The answer to a bottom's prayer.

Seriously, this is a winner:

> I always choose a Brownlong chair,
> The seat that's neat and made with care.
>
> (*flair?*)

But Adam had a better idea. He sat down at the desk and took out the sepia postcard of the British Museum which he had purchased that afternoon. He addressed it to Brownlong & Co., and stamped it, ready to be posted on the way home. The Reading Room was almost empty, and an official lingered impatiently near Adam, waiting for him to leave. But Adam refused to be hurried as he penned his couplet in a bold, clear script. He leaned back and regarded it with satisfaction. It had the hard-edged clarity of a good imagist lyric, the subtle reverberations of a fine *haiku*, the economy of a classic epigram.

> I always choose a Brownlong chair,
> Because it's stuffed with pubic hair.

Adam drove slowly along the Embankment, straining his eyes for the sight of a convenient pillar-box – convenient in this instance meaning one he could reach without getting off his scooter and stalling the engine. The noises coming from the engine were getting increasingly ugly – all this travelling in low gear had taken its toll – and he was not confident that, once stopped, it would ever start again.

Posting his contribution to the Brownlong competition had

become a matter of some importance to him, the completion of his one, small achievement of the day. No, that wasn't quite true – he had the manuscript of *Robert and Rachel* snugly tucked away in the tool compartment of his scooter, swaddled tenderly in his college scarf. But, interesting as it was, he was growing increasingly doubtful that he would be able to turn it to his own advantage. Someone – Mrs Rottingdean presumably – held the copyright, and she was clearly not going to let him publish it. Perhaps she could even prevent him from reporting on it – he was uncertain about such legal technicalities. Furthermore, he had inadvertently brought away with him from Bayswater the manuscript of *Lay Sermons and Private Prayers* and he would have to find some way of returning it to Mrs Rottingdean before she put the Metropolitan Police on his trail.

The sudden blast of a fog-horn – just behind his left ear, it seemed – made him jump. It was a real pea-souper down here by the river. The atmosphere seemed to be compounded of equal portions of moisture and soot. A faint smell of burning stung his nose and throat – it was as if the whole city were gently smouldering.

He found a pillar-box at last, and drew up beside it. Grasping the throttle of his scooter with his right hand, he leaned out to post the card with his left. But the slit was on the opposite side of the pillar-box and he lost his balance momentarily, dropping the card and losing his grip on the scooter, the engine of which promptly died. Cursing, Adam retrieved the card and posted it. Then he girded himself to push the scooter into life again. It was still a long walk to home, and he was very tired. Please God let it fire, he prayed, as he began to run.

The engine fired all right; in fact, it burst into flames. They licked greedily at Adam's ankles, and he jumped clear, allowing the scooter to proceed alone for several yards, a miniature fire-ship, before it toppled over into the gutter. He ran after it and tore his bags from the luggage grid. Aware of the danger of an explosion, he retreated to a safe distance with his bags, then remembered, with a spasm of horror, the manuscript of *Robert and Rachel*. He hurried back to the scooter and, screening his face from the heat, pried open the lid of the tool compartment. A jet of flame shot up and singed his duffle coat. He reeled back. Too late! Egbert Merrymarsh's lost masterpiece had perished in its second ordeal by fire.

There was a loud explosion. The scooter arched into the air like a creature in its final agony; it crashed to the ground, a twisted heap of blazing metal, and after two last convulsive jerks and a muted wail from its horn, expired.

There was total silence except for the brisk crackling of flames and the sympathetic lamentation of fog-horns from downstream. Adam stood stunned, waiting for the policemen, the firemen, the bystanders to assemble. But no one came. At last a dog limped out of the fog and lay down before the pyre, licking its chops appreciatively. Adam picked up his bags and prepared to walk. His legs felt weak and he staggered slightly. He heard, rather than saw, a large car draw up at the kerbside. A door opened and shut.

'Hi there,' said a familiar voice. 'Having trouble?'

'Oh, hallo,' said Adam. 'I've got a message for you.'

'Drink?' inquired the American, pulling down a flap behind the driver's partition and revealing a row of bottles.

'I'd love one,' said Adam, sinking into the soft grey upholstery. The limousine was purring slowly along the Embankment, but the blinds were drawn inside and he had no sensation of movement. Soothing music was coming from a speaker concealed somewhere behind his seat.

'Scotch, Bourbon, gin, Cognac?'

'Cognac, please.'

The fat American poured a generous measure of brandy into

a huge balloon glass and handed it to Adam. 'That should give you a lift. Tough break, your scooter catching fire. Still, it's insured I guess?'

'I hadn't thought of that,' said Adam, brightening.

'So what was that about a message?' said the fat American, opening a bottle of whisky.

'Oh, yes, someone phoned from Colorado – I got the message by mistake. Something about a hundred thousand for books and fifty thousand for manuscripts. Or was it the other way round . . .'

The American uttered a sigh of impatience. 'Those guys think too small,' he said. He splashed soda in his glass and Adam heard the chink of ice. 'Well, here's to our third meeting today –'

'Fourth,' said Adam.

'How's that?'

'Wasn't it you this afternoon on the gallery in the Reading Room?'

'Geeze, was that you? What were you doing up there?'

'I was running away.'

'Is that right? And I was running away from you . . . Well, here's to our fourth meeting, then. And the Summit College Library.'

'Here's to them,' said Adam. They drank.

'Say, I forgot to ask, where do you live, Adam?'

'Battersea.'

The American slid back the glass partition and spoke to his chauffeur. 'You know where Battersea is?'

'Yes, sir.'

'Well, that's where we're going.'

'Right, sir.'

'That's very kind of you, Mr, er . . .'

'You're welcome. Schnitz is the name, but call me Bernie.'

'I hope the fog –'

'Don't worry about the fog. I think he has radar in the front there. This car's got damn near everything else.'

'It's marvellous,' said Adam, sipping his brandy. Emboldened by the liquor, he put a question:

'What were you doing in the Reading Room, then . . . Bernie?'

'I figured I'd take advantage of the confusion to really examine the structure of the building . . .'

'The structure?'

'Yeah, it's like this, I had this great idea, a vision, you might call it. I was going to buy the British Museum and transport it stone by stone to Colorado, clean it up and re-erect it.'

Adam boggled. 'With all the books?'

'Yeah, you see we have this little College in Colorado, high up in the Rockies – highest school in the world as a matter of fact, we have to have oxygen on tap in every room . . . Well, it's a fine place, but we're not expanding as we should be – you know, we're not getting the good students, the top teachers. So I told the trustees what was needed: a real class library – rare books, original manuscripts, that sort of thing. "OK Bernie," they said, "go to Europe and get us a library." So I came to the best library in the world.'

'I don't think it's for sale, somehow,' Adam said.

'No, I guess you're right. I hadn't figured on it being that big,' said Bernie, sadly. Adam almost shared his regret. It was a thrilling vision he had conjured up, of the B.M. scoured of its soot and pigeon droppings, its tall pillars and great dome gleaming in their pristine glory, starkly outlined against the blue Colorado sky at the summit of some craggy mountain. 'Never mind,' he said consolingly. 'With all that money, you'll be able to buy a good collection.'

'Yeah, but I haven't the time to buy it in bits and pieces. Hunting for manuscripts especially – you've no idea the time it takes.'

'I've got an original manuscript with me, by an odd chance,' said Adam. 'But I don't think it would interest you.'

'Let's have a look at it, Adam.'

Adam took *Lay Sermons and Private Prayers* out of one of his bags and passed it over. 'It's very boring and of no literary merit whatsoever,' he said, as Bernie thumbed through the manuscript.

'Was this ever published?'

'No. Merrymarsh published a number of books, but he couldn't get anyone to take that.'

'Well, we will,' said Bernie. 'How much do you want for it?'

'It's not mine,' said Adam. 'The owner wants £250 for it.'

'Let's say two seventy-five,' said Bernie. 'You're entitled to a commission.' He took out a thick wad of five-pound notes and began counting them into Adam's hand. Adam stopped him at the fifth.

'Would you mind paying the owner direct?' he said. 'You'll find her name and address on the inside of the cover.'

'OK,' said Bernie. 'Say, Adam, could you use a part-time job?'

'What kind of job?'

'Scouting for books and manuscripts for our library. It's like this: I have to go back to the States soon. You could be our buyer on the spot. Ten per cent commission and expenses. Is it a deal?'

'I think so,' said Adam. 'But I'll have to ask my wife.'

Bernie dropped Adam at the corner of his street. As they shook hands, he pressed a card into Adam's.

'This is my hotel. Call me when you've talked to your wife.'

Adam bounded down the street, indifferent to the bags banging against his knees. He was going to do more than talk to his wife. He was going to make love to her.

He paused at the gate and looked up at the window of their bedroom. The light was on, so she wasn't asleep yet. Was that a star he could see above the roof . . .? The fog was clearing then. And, yes – he flexed his leg – he had lost his limp. It was absurd to let this pregnancy thing get on top of you. If she was, they might as well make the best of it, and if she wasn't –

His elation subsided as he suddenly thought of something. Supposing . . . supposing, since he had last spoken to her . . . supposing . . .

It was absurd, but he actually hoped her period hadn't started.

Epilogue

Perhaps she ought to wake Adam up and tell him it had started, Barbara thought, as she came out of the bathroom. The passage was quite dark but, schooled by many night-time alarms and excursions, she negotiated it with confidence. Their bedroom was dimly lit by the street lamps shining through the curtains, and Adam's face had a bluish tint. He was sound asleep. She wasn't surprised – by the sound of it he'd been tearing all over London all day in the fog; and she wouldn't be surprised if he'd been drunk at the sherry party. That was probably how he lost his job, she speculated. The job he never had. They were going to give it to Camel, apparently. Well, Camel had waited long enough. And this offer by the American sounded all right, if she'd got it straight.

'Adam,' she said softly, as she took off her dressing-gown. But he didn't stir. Let him sleep, then. Tomorrow would be soon enough to tell him. And wouldn't he be pleased. Rush off to the Museum full of beans. He never could work properly when he was worried, which meant once a month at least . . .

As she was getting into bed Barbara heard a muffled cry. Dominic. Resignedly she swung her feet to the floor again and pushed them into her slippers. She shrugged on her dressing-gown and padded into the children's room. Dominic had managed to roll his sheets into ropes and had got them knotted round his legs. She held the whimpering child in one arm while she smoothed the bedclothes with her other hand. As she tucked him up again he fell into a deep and peaceful sleep. Barbara glanced at Edward. From the shadows came Clare's voice: 'Can I have a drink of water, Mummy?'

'Why aren't you asleep, Clare?'

'I'm thirsty.'

'All right.'

Barbara fetched a glass of water from the kitchen. Clare sipped it slowly.

'Is Daddy back?'

'Yes, dear.'

'Where's Daddy's uniform, Mummy?'

'What do you mean?'

'The men who worked at the British Museum had uniforms.'

'Daddy doesn't do that kind of work.'

'What kind of –'

'Shsh. Go to sleep. It's late.'

Well, the children had enjoyed the trip to the Museum, anyway. Still, it had been silly of her to panic like that. What good would it have done, supposing there *had* been a fire? He might have been trying to reach her by telephone. Goodness, he must have spent a fortune in phone calls today. And what had he been doing all the afternoon, anyway? Oh, she hadn't heard the whole story yet, not by a long chalk.

A ruck in the curtains attracted her notice, and she went over to the window to adjust them. Well, he'd nearly burned himself to death anyway, by all accounts, she thought, looking out of the window and catching sight of the crumpled tarpaulin in the garden below. Funny that the scooter had never given any trouble while Dad had it. Perhaps he didn't know how to drive it properly. Who ever heard of a scooter catching fire spontaneously? She wasn't sorry though – he was bound to have killed himself on it one of these days, and the insurance would come in handy. With the money the American had given him, they would be quite rich for a while.

I need a new coat, she thought, as she returned to the kitchen with the half-filled glass. My red one is all out of shape from carrying Dominic and Edward. I'll get a fitted one this time. Act of faith, but I might as well make the most of my figure while I've still got it. Shoes for Dominic. A blouse for Clare. And underpants for Adam, four pairs at least. Can't have that happening again. I had to laugh when he took off his trousers tonight, I'd forgotten all about it. Supposing you had an accident, as Mum used to say. As if it was all right to have an accident as long as your underwear was respectable.

Barbara emptied the glass at the sink and filled it again to drink herself. This morning he remembered that day in France, she thought, that day we went swimming in our underclothes and afterwards I didn't wear anything under my dress. The sea and the sun and miles from home. That was the nearest we ever came to . . . Good job we didn't. With our luck we'd have had to get married straight away. Have six children now instead of three. Poor Mary Flynn. What will it be? Five all under six. I'd go mad, literally stark staring mad. Damn, I've forgotten to lay the table for breakfast.

With quiet, deft movements Barbara spread a cloth on the table, and began to lay out knives, forks, spoons, cups and saucers, plates, cornflakes and marmalade.

Why I forgot was because he was so keen to get into bed, she thought. But I like it when we make love spontaneously. That's the trouble with the Safe Method, or one of them, it's too mechanical, you're always watching the calendar, it's like launching a rocket – five four three two one, and by the time it's zero you're too tensed up to . . . Not tonight, though. I've not known him so happy for ages, bubbling over with plans for finishing his thesis and finding old books and manuscripts for the American and what was it he said about writing a novel, as if he hadn't got enough on his plate. Probably have forgotten all about it by the morning.

Her eyes were now quite accustomed to the darkness, and it had become in an odd way a point of honour not to switch on the light. She felt delicately in the dark recesses of drawers and cupboards for the things she wanted, taking pleasure in this testing of her sense of touch.

I'll feel awful telling Mary I'm not pregnant after all, she thought. If she hadn't converted her husband they would have been able to use contraceptives. Doesn't seem fair, somehow. Lots of girls marry non-Catholics on purpose. He has to sign a promise, but if he goes back on it and insists the priest will tell you to submit for the sake of saving the marriage. It's the lesser evil, they say, but it only applies if the Catholic partner's a woman. That's typical – as if they never dreamed a woman might want to insist. Perhaps they wouldn't have when they made the rule. The Vatican's always about a hundred years out of date.

Barbara yawned and shivered. She made a last check on the breakfast table, and left the kitchen.

And another thing I've forgotten is to say my prayers, she thought, as she reached the bedroom. Perhaps I'll skip them tonight. But I suppose I've got something to be thankful for. Just a Hail Mary then. There's such a draught across this floor.

Hail Mary, full of grace, the Lord is with thee, blessed art thou amongst women and blessed is the fruit of thy womb perhaps I should tell Adam now. If he wakes before me in the morning he'll lie there all depressed wondering if I'm pregnant. But perhaps he'll see the box on the dressing-table and guess. Wasn't there some French woman who used to change the flower in her bosom from white to red to tip off her lovers? Was it *La Dame aux Camélias*? I don't know. I'm forgetting all my French lit. But they're white and red. The language of flowers. Better than some ways of saying it, like the curse, or what is it they say in Birmingham, 'I haven't seen yet this month.' And that American girl, what was her name, in my last year at college, said falling off a roof. Well, Clare will say period and menstruate if I have anything to do with it. And I'll make sure she knows in good time, not like me up in the bedroom screaming I'm dying, I've never forgiven Mum for that. Or that poor girl, what was her name, Olive in IIIA, Olive Green, couldn't forget a name like that, bad as Adam Appleby. She went up to the teacher in class, 'Please Miss, I've got a terrible headache.' Teacher thought she meant period and gave her a sanitary towel to put on. She came back from the cloakroom half an hour later wearing it round her head, never seen one in her life before. Funny thing was, nobody laughed, though girls are little beasts at that age. Who was that teacher? Miss Bassett, she taught us French and History. It was she who encouraged me to do French at the University. The main attraction was the six months in France, but I'd met Adam by then and I didn't want to go. He was almost out of his mind, wrote to me every day till he couldn't stand it any longer he hitch-hiked right down to the South of France and we decided to get engaged. I'll never forget the day he turned up out of the blue on Madame Gerard's front door step sweating and covered in dust when he took off his rucksack he couldn't straighten up he had to turn sideways and sort of twist his head round to talk to her. I believe she thought he was a tramp his French was incomprehensible a good job I was there or perhaps she would have slammed the door on him not that she was any more pleased when she found out who he was she was a sour old shrew seemed to think my chastity was her personal responsibility chaperoned us all the time except that one day she had to go into Perpignan and we went to the sea . . .

This is no good, I'm falling asleep. Thank you God for not letting me be pregnant. There, that's short and sweet and from the heart. Let's get into bed. Ah. Ooh. My feet are like blocks of ice. I wonder if it will disturb him if I just put my foot just under his knee just there, ah, that's better. Hallo, he's stirring, ow, ouch my leg! Have to make him cut his toenails tomorrow, like having another baby to look after, I must stop Clare getting hold of the scissors, if only he would put a hook in high up somewhere, but if you tell him anything he doesn't listen, comes of having to study in a house full of children. He says if I train myself not to hear the constant racket you can't expect me to hear you and not the children. Perhaps he'll improve if we get a bigger flat or better still a house with a garden, somewhere for the children to let off steam, but I doubt it, he's always in a dream, what was it he said, a novel where life kept taking the shape of literature, did you ever hear anything so cracked, life is life and books are books and if he was a woman he wouldn't need to be told that.

Whooooo there goes another fog-horn, they sound so close, such a melancholy sound, reminds me of when he came to see me off at Dover, standing at the quayside with his hands in his pockets trying to shout something, but every time he opened his mouth the hooter went, and of course it had to be a great handsome French boy who was at the rail beside me I never even spoke to him but he couldn't sleep that night for jealousy he said in his letter funny how jealous he was before we were married well that's one foot thawed out let's try the other ah that's nice he always so warm after we so am I but getting out of bed spoils it perhaps that's what started it off that's happened before our honeymoon was the first time three days early instead of late the last one for about two years too what a honeymoon that was but how was I to know it would be early I suppose that's why they let the girl name the day funny I never thought of that before I didn't have any choice it was his embarkation leave and I thought it would be a safe period anyway it was safe all night after that the sheets looked like a battle had passed over he nearly had a fit the next morning wanted to smuggle them out pretend we'd lost them settle for a new pair as if hotels weren't used to he never could stand the sight of blood nearly has kittens if the children cut themselves I suppose I'll end up putting that hook in myself I seem to lose so much blood since I had Dominic perhaps I could get some pills from the doctor to reduce it but they might upset my cycle that's another thing against the safe method there are so many other things that can affect ovulation

there was a great list of them in that book what it was change
of environment change of diet illness height above sea level
emotional disturbance no wonder they called it Vatican Roulette
what is love itself but emotional disturbance perhaps this temperature business is the answer this is the third or is it the fourth
month it's worked the trouble is though once you've had a failure
with any so called safe method Safe method that's a laugh
Rhythm isn't much better funny sort of rhythm one week on
three weeks off that American girl Jean something was her name
Jean Kaufman said once a boy took her to the Rhode Island
Rhythm Centre thinking it was a jazz club and taking your
temperature every morning that's a bore Mary said she's tried
everything including temperature charts she's one of the unlucky
ones it won't work for so what is she supposed to do I'd like to
know O the Church will have to change its attitude there's no
doubt about that and if I was in her place I wouldn't wait there's
many in mine who wouldn't come to that they say there's a huge
number of Catholics it was in that article he showed me he says
the Church is bound to change soon and won't there be an
uproar from the older generation you can see it already in the
Catholic papers dear sir I have no patience with the moans of
young couples today who put a car and washing machine above
the responsibilities of parenthood we have been poor but happy
all our lives God always provides mother of nine can't blame
them really for feeling they've had a rough deal mum told me
when she was young even the safe method was frowned on and
you were only supposed to use it if you were starving or going
to die from another pregnancy the trouble is this myth of the
large family what's so marvellous about a large family I'd like to
know there was only one child in the Holy Family six in ours
and we were at each other's throats most of the time who's that
Dominic don't say I've got to get out again no he's stopped only
a dream I don't want any more three would suit me fine ha some
hopes how many years to my menopause could be fifteen years

my God and that's when a lot of women have one because they think and I don't suppose the temperature charts any use then either it's like lactation that's how lactation ovulation basal temperature you get to sound like a doctor after a while that's how Mary had her second funny how many people think you can't conceive while you're breast feeding safe method doesn't work then either so it doesn't encourage you to breast feed but breast feedings natural so much for the natural law if you ask me nobody gives a damn for the natural law the only reason well perhaps it is the natural law in a way there's something a bit off putting about contraceptives even non-Catholics would prefer not to I don't suppose I'd jump for joy if the Pope said it was all right tomorrow don't like the idea of pushing a bit of rubber and what's that jelly stuff spermicide Moses the name alone is enough to turn you off and they aren't 100 per cent reliable anyway surprising the number of non-Catholics who I bet if we decided to use them now that would happen to us wouldn't that be great perhaps the only way to be perfectly sure would be to combine it with the temperature chart my God you could spend your whole life preparing to get into bed if you let yourself perhaps the pill is the answer but they say it makes you drowsy and other side effects there's always a snag perhaps that's the root of the matter there's something about sex perhaps it's original sin I don't know but we'll never get it neatly tied up you think you've got it under control in one place it pops up in another either it's comic or tragic nobody's immune you see some couple going off to the Continent in their new sports car and envy them like hell next thing you find out they're dying to have a baby those who can't have them want them those who have them don't want them or not so many of them everyone has problems if you only knew Sally Pond was round the other day who'd have guessed she was frigid because of that man when she was nine can't do it unless she's had a couple of stiff drinks got completely stewed the other night she said and bit George

in the leg now she's seeing a psychiatrist it makes you wonder
if there's such a thing as a normal sexual relationship I don't
think there is if you mean by normal no problems embarrass-
ments disappointments there always are not that that entitles
the church to sit back and say put up with it can be wonderful
too and there are times when married people have to ought to
and it isn't always a safe period either like when Adam was in
the army that's how we had Dominic well perhaps the church
will change and a good thing too there'll be much less misery
in the world but it's silly to think that everything in the garden
will be lovely it won't it never is I think I always knew that before
we were married perhaps every woman does how could we put
up with menstruation pregnancy and everything otherwise not
like men he has this illusion that it's only the birth control
business which stops him from getting sex perfectly under
control it's like his thesis he keeps saying if only I could get my
notes in the right order the thesis would write itself what was
that he said suddenly when I thought he'd fallen asleep I've
realized what the longest sentence in English fiction is I wonder
what it is he had such an idealist view of marriage when we were
courting I don't think he's recovered from the shock yet though
I warned him perhaps he didn't listen to what I said then either
even that day at the sea I remember I suppose you could say that
was when he proposed though we'd assumed it for some time
I wasn't as starry-eyed as he was though I was pretty carried
away I admit that beach with not a soul in sight we bicycled for
miles to find it because we'd forgotten our costumes and we
went swimming in our underwear his pants were inside out I
remember that's typical we spread our things on the sand to dry
the trees came down to the beach we sat in the shade and ate
the sandwiches and drank the wine the footprints in the sand
were only ours the sea was empty it was like a desert island we
lay down he took me in his arms shall we come back here when
we're married he said perhaps I said he held me low down tight

against him we'll make love in this same spot he said my dress was so thin I could feel him hard against me perhaps we'll have children with us I said then we'll come down at night he said perhaps we won't be able to afford to come at all I said you're not very optimistic he said perhaps it's better not to be I said I'm going to be famous and earn lots of money he said perhaps you won't love me then I said I'll always love you he said I'll prove it every night he kissed my throat perhaps you think that now I said but I couldn't keep it up perhaps we will be happy I said of course we will he said we'll have a nanny to look after the children perhaps we will I said by the way how many children are we going to have as many as you like he said it'll be wonderful you'll see perhaps it will I said perhaps it will be wonderful perhaps even though it won't be like you think perhaps that won't matter perhaps.

PENGUIN DECADES

Penguin Decades bring you the novels that helped shape modern Britain. When they were published, some were bestsellers, some were considered scandalous, and others were simply misunderstood. All represent their time and helped define their generation, while today each is considered a landmark work of storytelling. Each is introduced by a modern admirer.

50s
Scenes from Provincial Life/William Cooper (1950) Nick Hornby
Lucky Jim/Kingsley Amis (1954) David Nicholls
The Chrysalids/ John Wyndham (1955) M. John Harrison
From Russia with Love/Ian Fleming (1957) Christopher Andrew
Billy Liar/Keith Waterhouse (1959) Blake Morrison

60s
A Clockwork Orange/Anthony Burgess (1962) Will Self
The Millstone/Margaret Drabble (1965) Elaine Showalter
The British Museum is Falling Down/David Lodge (1965) Mark Lawson
A Kestrel for a Knave/Barry Hines (1968) Ian McMillan
Another Part of the Wood/Beryl Bainbridge (1969) Lynn Barber

70s
I'm the King of the Castle/Susan Hill (1970) Esther Freud
Don't Look Now/Daphne du Maurier (1971) Julie Myerson
The Infernal Desire Machines of Doctor Hoffman/Angela Carter (1972) Ali Smith
The Children of Dynmouth/William Trevor (1976) Roy Foster
Treasures of Time/Penelope Lively (1979) Selina Hastings

80s
A Month in the Country/J. L. Carr (1980) Byron Rogers
An Ice-Cream War/William Boyd (1982) Giles Foden
Hawksmoor/Peter Ackroyd (1985) Will Self
Paradise Postponed/John Mortimer (1985) Jeremy Paxman
Latecomers/Anita Brookner (1988) Helen Dunmore

Decades 1960s

The 1960s was the decade of social revolution, anti-war protests, liberal reforms, civil rights and psychedelia. Skirts got shorter and hair got longer, London swung, the Berlin Wall went up, a man walked on the moon, the Beatles and the Rolling Stones reigned and England even won the World Cup.

A Clockwork Orange/Anthony Burgess (1962)
'It was Burgess's genius to catch a particular kind of wave – a demographic one; for, as the   baby boom exploded into affluence, throughout the 1960s, 70s and 80s, so the formerly contained have-nots became a vast tribal confederation of wanna-haves' – Will Self

The Millstone/Margaret Drabble (1965)
'While *The Millstone* can be read as social realism and an investigation of the conditions of maternity in England in the 1960s, it can also be read as a timeless fable about the condition of womanhood and the relation between mother and child … Margaret Drabble's vision of woman's fate remains challenging, controversial, relevant and profound' – Elaine Showalter

The British Museum is Falling Down/David Lodge (1965)
'In *The British Museum is Falling Down*, a novel packed with shadowings of language, David Lodge did the linguistic double: Catholic and catholic, this winning comedy of "Vatican Roulette" gives parochial concerns a universal appeal' – Mark Lawson

A Kestrel for a Knave/Barry Hines (1968)
'What the book has, in abundance, is poetry... Hines's idea, rooted in his viscerally felt politics, is that we should all be available for beauty and available for change'– Ian McMillan

Another Part of the Wood/Beryl Bainbridge (1969)
'Like all Bainbridge's novels, *Another Part of the Wood* sets off at a cracking pace, and never slows down … It repays double reading – once, quickly, to solve the dreadful suspense, and then again, slowly, to enjoy its sly rich subtlety' – Lynn Barber

He just wanted a decent
book to read ...

Not too much to ask, is it? It was in 1935 when Allen Lane, Managing
Director of Bodley Head Publishers, stood on a platform at Exeter railway
station looking for something good to read on his journey back to London.
His choice was limited to popular magazines and poor-quality paperbacks –
the same choice faced every day by the vast majority of readers, few of
whom could afford hardbacks. Lane's disappointment and subsequent anger
at the range of books generally available led him to found a company – and
change the world.

*'We believed in the existence in this country of a vast reading public for intelligent
books at a low price, and staked everything on it'*
Sir Allen Lane, 1902–1970, founder of Penguin Books

The quality paperback had arrived – and not just in bookshops. Lane was
adamant that his Penguins should appear in chain stores and tobacconists,
and should cost no more than a packet of cigarettes.

Reading habits (and cigarette prices) have changed since 1935, but
Penguin still believes in publishing the best books for everybody to
enjoy. We still believe that good design costs no more than bad design,
and we still believe that quality books published passionately and responsibly
make the world a better place.

So wherever you see the little bird – whether it's on a piece of
prize-winning literary fiction or a celebrity autobiography, political tour
de force or historical masterpiece, a serial-killer thriller, reference book,
world classic or a piece of pure escapism – you can bet that it represents
the very best that the genre has to offer.

Whatever you like to read – trust Penguin.